Alwa[illegible] Amy

LOVE ALWAYS BOOK TWO

Always, Amy

BELINDA MARY

H&J Publishing

Cover Illustrations by Lorissa Padilla Designs

1st edition 2023

ISBN: 978-0-6456942-3-9

www.belindamary.com

For those who have had their heart bruised,
And are brave enough to fall in love again.

CONTENTS

Please note this book is based in Australia, written by an Australian author, in Australian English. Words may appear to be spelt incorrectly, but that is just the way we do it down here! Enjoy!

Content warning: Some cheating described, not between FMC and MMC.

PROLOGUE

Lucas

Two Years Ago

I SPOT HER INSTANTLY. THOUGH the room is dark and crowded and she's surrounded by people, to me it feels like there's a spotlight just on her. I can't tear my eyes away. Long brown hair shimmering in these dim lights and a bright smile. She is stunning. I watch her dance with the group of women around her, attempting some sort of choreography, laughing without an ounce of self-consciousness, and I'm struck by an urgent need to meet her. What is this feeling?

I force myself to look away from her, out of fear of looking like some sort of stalker, and glance down at the glass in my hand. How much had I drunk this evening? Everything feels off-balance. Is this delayed jetlag? I arrived here from Florence over a week ago, so that doesn't seem plausible, but there needs to be some sort of explanation for these weird emotions I'm currently experiencing. My eyes unwittingly move back to her and seeing that she's walking toward the bar, without a conscious thought, I follow her. As I approach her, I see she is tall, but still only comes up to my collarbone, and she smells divine. *How can I smell her, crushed in amongst all these people?* I wonder to myself as I wait for her to turn around.

After she orders two vodkas with ice—a classic drink order—I open my mouth to wow her with a witty opening remark and come out with, "A vodka girl, hey?" Real smooth, Lucas. What's wrong with me?

The beautiful creature turns to me, and I'm struck dumb when I see her up close. A heart-shaped face, big light-brown eyes with golden flecks in them, like caramel. This close to her, I can see a smattering of freckles across her nose. She is perfection. She looks up at me, her mouth slightly agape, and then behind her, like she's confused who I'm talking to. *I'm talking to you, only you,* I want to tell her. Instead, I proceed with my amazing repertoire and say, "I'm Lucas."

Clearly not enamoured with my brilliant conversation starters, she continues to stare at me while I smile at her. I can't help myself; she's so delightful to look at. And as she takes her drinks from the bartender and appears to be leaving me, I act on instinct. Pointing to the drinks in her hand, I say, "Do you want to find somewhere quieter to drink those?" I wait with bated breath as she tilts her head and gives me a contemplative look. After what feels like an eternity, her perfectly pink lips lift in a half-smile and she nods her head. Grateful that she's agreed, I grab both of the glasses from her hands and walk to a quieter area of the bar, thankful when she follows me.

Once I've found us a place of our own, away from the crowds of people dancing and drinking, I attempt to get a conversation happening. Not something that usually requires this much effort, but there's something about this woman that's making me tongue-tied.

"I'm Amy," she finally says.

Amy. Yes.

As she continues to speak, and I attempt to join in the conversation, I'm distracted by everything about her. Her smile, the way she laughs, how her hand feels when she touches my arm. And that scent, it's driving me crazy. I have this intense desire to grab her face and kiss her, and as she continues chatting with me, leaning in closer, flirting with me in return, I think maybe she wouldn't mind if I did.

"So, what do you do?" Amy asks me now.

"I'm a doctor," I tell her, still filled with pride that this is my chosen career path. That I get to help people every single day still sends a thrill through me.

I watch the light go out of her eyes and think that maybe she doesn't feel the same way about my noble profession. She takes a rapid step away from me and I panic.

"What? What's wrong? What did I say?" I ask, desperate to fix whatever it is and have her stay here with me.

Amy mumbles something incoherent, and then she's gone. I watch, feeling helpless, as she sprints away from me, grabbing her friend and almost dragging her to the door. What just happened? Where's she going? As she disappears out the door, I get the sinking feeling that I just lost my chance with her. And I'm crushed by the realisation that I may never see her again.

CHAPTER 1

Amy

Two Years Later—Present Day

I WATCH MY BIG BROTHER get down on one knee and propose to my very choked-up, deliriously happy best friend, and smile. I couldn't be more ecstatic for the two of them. They finally got over themselves and chose a life together. As Lilly bursts into tears, also getting down on her knees to accept the proposal and squealing "yes!", I jump up and down in delight. They are such a good match. Oliver is the perfect balm for Lilly's particular brand of crazy, and Oliver is a lighter, more content version of himself when Lilly's around.

Once they've finished celebrating and have broken apart from their embrace, I grab two glasses of champagne and head over.

"Congratulations, my sister-in-law-to-be!" I yell, grabbing Lilly in a full-body bear hug.

With tears streaming down her face, she hugs me back, whispering, "I'm so happy."

Oliver joins us in the hug and the three of us do a little happy dance shuffle.

"You did good, big bro," I say, looking at the giant rock of an engagement ring that he has just put on to Lilly's finger. It's a large oval cut diamond, on a slim, yellow-gold band and it is beautiful. As she waves it in front of our faces, we both marvel at how sparkly it is.

"Now you'll officially be part of the family," I tell Lilly, who knows she's always been an honorary Harlow. As she grins at the thought, both Lilly's and my parents interrupt our conversation, all four of them wanting a piece of the future bride and groom.

I step back to give them some space and look around the room. Lilly's done such an amazing job getting this place to look exactly like what she had envisioned on her Pinterest board. The café is small, but she's made the space feel homey. Couches and an eclectic mix of mismatched chairs and tables fill the floor space, and on the walls, she's hung an array of photos of her family and friends. On every tabletop there rests a colourful vase filled with fresh native flowers and the overall effect is both funky and stylish. When Lilly first had the idea to open a café and bakery, she'd wanted it to feel comfortable, somewhere for people to catch up and hang out, and looking around now, I think that she got it spot on.

Spying a sample tray of brownies going around the room, I chase after the waitress, hoping to get one before they disappear. Lilly's baking business has expanded rapidly over the past six months, and with it, her baking prowess has grown tenfold. Everything she makes is next-level delicious. I manage to capture not one, but two treats for myself and head to a corner to enjoy them in solitude. After taking my first bite—*oh Lilly, these are so good they should be illegal*—I scan the patrons mingling about, ecstatic at the large turnout for this special occasion.

When I see Oliver's friend Dale across the room, flirting with our friend Sammi, I give him a nod and continue my perusal. And then I see him. Him. No, that can't be right. He isn't even in the country. Last I heard, he was still in Florence. I rub my eyes to check that my mind isn't playing tricks on me. It *is* him. Lucas freaking Mancini is here, in the flesh, and he's walking toward me. I'm not ready.

To avoid eye contact and hopefully delay this inevitable meeting, I look around for the exit with desperation. Which is right behind him. I'm frantic now, trying and failing to think of a way to make myself invisible—

"Amy," comes his deep voice from right in front of me.

I steel my spine, knowing that any chance to escape is long gone, and look up at him. And look up and up some more. In the twelve months he has been gone, I'd forgotten how tall he is. And how mouth-wateringly good-looking. With his deep blue eyes and his stupid chiselled jaw, he's like one of Lilly's desserts. So good he should be illegal.

"Lucas," I say, proud that my voice is steady. "What are you doing here?"

"I follow Lilly on Instagram and saw that she's having her grand opening today. I wanted to come and congratulate her, and to see you—"

Before he can finish that sentence, I cut him off. "When did you get back?"

He gives me a strange look before answering. "I've been back a few weeks. Didn't you get my messages?"

He must be unaware that I blocked his number and muted all of his social media accounts the minute he walked out the door all those months ago.

"I must have missed them. I've been pretty busy, you know..." I trail off as Lucas reaches out to touch my arm, only to stop when

I take a hasty step backward. "Anyway, it's good to see you," I lie. "But I have to get back to my family. It's a big day for all of us."

Lucas smiles at me, though his eyes are shadowed with sadness. "I'm so glad those two worked things out," he says, nodding to where Lilly and Oliver are slowly dancing together to no music. "I know how much you wanted them together."

I wince thinking of the night I confided in him, the night of Lilly's twenty-fourth birthday when I left the bar with him, right before his abrupt departure. The night I rarely let myself think about anymore.

"Yes, they got their happy ending." I start to move away from him now, proud that I got through this conversation without breaking down and come to a stop when I hear him say from behind me.

"I missed you, Amy."

Faltering for a moment, I only just resist the urge to turn back to him, not wanting to give him the satisfaction of knowing the impact of those words. And with my head held high, I walk away. He doesn't need to know just how much I've missed him, too.

I walk at pace away from the man I'd vowed never to speak to again—that didn't last, did it?—and try to grab the attention of Lilly, who's still basking in her loved-up glow, standing pressed up against Oliver with a cupcake in one hand, admiring her new ring on the other. Wildly waving my hands to get her to notice my dilemma, I attract an audience with my mother instead.

"Darling, what're you doing over here? Is this some new dance move the kids are doing these days? From that TikTok place?" Mum asks, forever trying to appear cool and "with it."

I put my arms down from where they've been flailing around, glancing over to make sure a certain someone isn't watching me—

good, he's too busy sampling the desserts to have caught my antics—and sigh.

"No, Mum. No dance moves here. Just stretching." I do an exaggerated side-stretch to give my cover some credence.

Mum gives me a doubtful look and then dives into a discussion I knew was coming my way, the minute I saw Oliver get down on one knee.

"So, are you seeing anyone special at the moment?"

Groan. As much as I love my mother who, along with my dad, has always been good to me and my brother, her incessant need to have me in a steady relationship—preferably married—has long been a point of contention between us.

"Not really, Mum. As you know from our weekly conversations, I've been pretty busy at work. Remember…? I'm working toward that promotion, the Chief Nursing Officer position? So, I haven't had too much time to focus on my love life."

Mum nods with understanding and I think I may have dodged a bullet when Dad strolls over to join the conversation.

"And when are we going to see you engaged, Amy Loo? Any young men that I need to be approving of? Anyone coming to ask me for your hand?" he says in his megaphone voice.

I glance around again, noticing that people are looking our way and smiling—or laughing—at us indulgently, and pray that Lucas is out of earshot.

"Dad! You're so embarrassing! As I was just telling Mum, I'm too busy at the moment to worry about my love life. And also, welcome back from the Stone Age—women no longer need the approval of their fathers to get married," I tell him with stern affection.

At this, my parents laugh and the conversation moves away from my non-existent love life for the moment. I know that this is just a temporary reprieve, as my parents are of that generation that believes a young lady needs a man in her life to be happy. I'm of the better and more evolved generation that knows this isn't the case. That a young woman can be happy alone, as long as she's got good friends, a good book and a good bottle of wine.

With these thoughts in my head, I tell my parents I'll catch up with them later, as they will only be in town a few days and I want to spend more time with them. When I am less emotionally rattled. And then I move, with stealth, toward Lilly, keeping a wary eye on Lucas as I go. After the many girl-talk sessions we had when she and Oliver were bumbling toward their happily ever after, she owes me.

"Ames!" Lilly slurs at me, pulling me in by the neck for an awkward, drunken hug. "I love you!"

Tipsy Lilly loves everyone.

"Yes, I love you too. Are you able to focus your champagne-bubble eyes across the room for a moment, and tell me what you see?"

She hums under her breath as she follows my instructions, her head coming to a cartoonish whiplash halt when she spots Lucas.

"What's *he* doing here?" she whisper-shouts.

I pull her to the other side of the room, as far away from Lucas as this small café space allows.

"He said he follows you on Instagram and wanted to come to your grand opening."

When Lilly doesn't immediately respond, I look at her to see she's staring at Lucas in that dazed way that women always do when he's around. With his commanding six-foot-three frame and dark features, he's a woman magnet.

"Lilly!" I snap my fingers in front of her face, getting her to focus. "What am I going to do with this new information?" I wave my hand in his direction, knowing that she'll understand my meaning.

"You mean the fact that he's back in the same country—nay, the same city as you?" Bingo, Lilly. You've got it.

"Yes! We're supposed to have half a world between us. And now, he's just here."

She looks at me with concern, knowing just what this means to me. That Lucas, with all of his charm and good looks, is my weakness.

"You guys haven't spoken at all since he left?" she clarifies.

I shake my head no. "He left. And I needed to be done with him. And now it appears that he's not only back, but he's back in my world."

"I wonder what it means?" she asks the obvious question out loud. "That he's here today? Did you speak to him?"

I look to where Lucas is standing, now chatting with Oliver—the traitor—and tell Lilly about our brief conversation.

"He said he missed you?" she asks, her glassy eyes wide as saucers. "What does that mean?"

"It means he's back to mess with my emotions again. Only this time it won't work. I have hardened my heart to the likes of him. It's the Alcatraz of hearts, completely impenetrable."

"I think you have your historical references wrong there, Ames. Isn't that the prison where no one could escape?" she says, getting us sidetracked.

"Hmmm, yes. But it still works. If no one can escape, then no one can get in. And that's my heart. A locked-down fortress."

At this, she looks at me sadly but knows better than to attempt to change my mind. I can be very stubborn when I set my mind to it, and Lilly is all too aware of this trait.

"OK, well, if your heart is safe from the likes of him, then just ignore him. Or better yet, treat him like you would treat any stranger, with polite kindness. That will show him he's no one to you now."

When did Lilly get so wise? I think, as I watch her sway softly to music that only she can hear. OK, maybe she isn't quite the Dalai Lama yet, but this is good advice. If I must interact with him, which let's face it is unlikely given this event is almost over, I'll kill him with kindness. He'll never know what he meant to me. And how long it took for me to put him behind me. Because that's where he is, in my past. And after today, that's where he will stay.

"Thanks, Lil. You can go back to your fiancé over there and enjoy the rest of your special day. I'm so proud of everything you've built here," I tell her with complete sincerity. "And I cannot wait for you to marry my brother and become my sister for real."

Lilly gives me a beaming smile, one that lights up her entire beautiful face, and pulls me in for a big hug.

"Thank you, bestie. I know Oliver and I would never have made it here without some strong encouragement and, some may say, meddling from you. You're the best!"

I watch as she skips—yes, actually skips—back to Oliver and turn to go in search of another drink. Smack bang into a wall of muscle.

Lucas reaches out a hand to steady me, scorching my arm in the process and throwing me off-balance.

"Are you OK? You didn't see me here."

I cannot seem to catch a break today.

"I'm fine," I tell him in a stilted voice. Polite kindness, I remind myself. "I hope I didn't hurt you?"

Lucas's laugh holds something in it, something I can't place, and he says, "Not this time, Amy."

Huh? I take a step back to get a look at his face, noting that in the year we've been apart his hair has gotten greyer around the temples, only adding to his sex appeal, and try to read the meaning behind this cryptic statement.

"I'm just heading out now. I'll see you at the hospital on Monday." And with a funny little half-bow, he walks around me and out the front door, the merry bell that Lilly attached to it ringing ominously in his wake.

Monday? Did he just say Monday? At the hospital? With this bombshell going off systematically in my brain—MONDAY?—I grab another glass of champagne, hoping to drink the rest of the day away. And as I sip on what will be the first of many more drinks, I think, *What in the world does the week ahead have in store for me?*

CHAPTER 2

After fulfilling my own prophecy and spending the rest of the grand opening drinking my feelings, I find myself, to my utter embarrassment, in the back seat of my parents' car being driven home, feeling a little drunk and a lot miserable. I'm twenty-five years old and I still need a lift home from Mum and Dad. It's a sad day to be Amy.

As I enter the small townhouse I call home, I make my way into my living room, kicking off my ever-so-cute heels as I go. With a deep sigh, I sink into my oversized, comfortable couch and cover myself with my favourite throw blanket. It was quite the night. I can't believe that Lucas is here in my space and seemingly back in my life. My mind is revolting at the thought of it. Unable to focus on even some bad reality TV to distract myself, I rest my head on one of my colourful couch cushions and close my eyes, thinking back to that night. The night I met Lucas.

It was the weekend after Lilly's twenty-third birthday almost exactly two years ago. She was miserable. She'd just been dumped by her loser boyfriend, Sebastian—I never liked that guy—and I was forcing her to go out and enjoy herself. Poor Lilly. After much cajoling, and many vodka shots, I managed to get her up on the dance floor. Laughing as we attempted to recreate some of the latest TikTok moves, I looked up and saw him. Just sitting there at the bar, staring at me. The most beautiful man I had ever seen in real life. And maybe in my make-believe fantasy life as well. I tried my best to ignore him, because what would I do with a man who looked like that? And instead remained intent on ensuring that Lilly had a good time.

"I think I need another drink," she yelled into my ear. Drunken Lilly had no volume control. "Can you get it for me? Oliver is being the alcohol monitor tonight, and I've apparently hit my two-drinks-per-hour limit."

I rolled my eyes at this, whilst also hiding my grin. Oliver had always been overprotective of Lilly.

"Of course, birthday girl. I'll get you any drink you want. And any amount. Today's all about you."

Lilly beamed at me, slurping the rest of whatever concoction she had in her glass, handing it to me, and requesting another. Vodka. With ice. I made my way to the bar, dodging the clumsy dancers around me, and yelled the order to the bartender, who was looking harried and a little stressed out.

"An easy one for you," I told him with a big smile, hoping to brighten his night. "Two vodka straights in tall glasses. With lots of ice."

The bartender looked at me with gratitude, clearly sick of the complicated orders that had been coming his way, and got to work pouring our drinks.

"A vodka girl, I see," came a deep voice from behind me.

I froze, my body reacting to the sound of his voice before my mind could even fathom why. I turned and looked up. There he was. The beautiful man, in all his glory. Inches from my face, smiling at me like he was delighted to be talking to me.

Confused, I looked around to see if he was speaking to someone else.

"I'm Lucas," he said, bringing my attention back to him, confirming that he was, in fact, talking to me.

I looked back at him and I almost immediately had to look away again. He was the real-life version of every book boyfriend I'd ever imagined. Deep blue eyes, a chiselled jawline, black hair styled to look messy with a touch of grey at the temples. And his lips, so plump, smiling at *me*. And—Oh no. He had a gap in between his front two teeth. I groaned internally. I was such a sucker for a gap-toothed smile.

"Here are your drinks," the bartender said, saving me from my long appraisal of this model man in front of me.

I turned and paid for the drinks, hoping to gain my composure as I did so. When I turned back around, he was still there, looking at me patiently, like he had all the time in the world to be talking to me.

"Umm," was all that my usually quick-witted mind could come up with.

Lucas's smile grew at this, as he offered to find us a quiet place in the bar to chat. I pondered this for less than a second before nodding and, in a flash, he was walking to the far side of the bar. I followed close behind him, because how could I not? I mean, he was gorgeous...and he had my drinks.

"And you are?" he asked, speaking into my ear. Causing goosebumps to spread down my neck and take over the top part of my body. And rendering me speechless. Instead of answering him, I just stared at him helplessly. At his long eyelashes and his olive complexion. He was so gorgeous that I had become—temporarily, I hoped—mute. This could not be happening to me.

Lucas didn't seem concerned by this development. He rested his arm against the wall, seeming content to stare right back at me. This wasn't normal. Two strangers should not be able to just stand in silence and look at each other without it becoming weird. Should they?

I shook myself out of this weird daze I was in.

"I'm Amy," I said. At last.

"Amy," he repeated back to me with satisfaction, seeming to savour the word. "It's my pleasure to meet you."

Does he have an accent? I questioned silently, taking a big sip of my drink, hoping to gain enough liquid courage to find the power of speech again. Please don't let him be foreign. That would just make my fantasy man complete.

"So, Amy, tell me all about yourself."

I raised my eyebrow at him. He wanted to know about...me?

"How much time do you have?" I asked him with a smile, watching in amazement as his own smile grew. *Boy, those were some straight teeth he had. I wonder if he'd ever had braces.*

"I have all the time in the world," he told me, making my stomach do a big somersault.

"Ummm, well, my name is Amy," I said, like I was at a job interview, feeling so nervous that my name was the only fact that came to mind.

At this, he let out a laugh, his eyes crinkling as he watched me in amusement.

"I got that part already," he said, reaching out and touching my arm to move me out of the path of some determined dancers, causing so many more goose pimples to take residence where his fingers connected with my skin. "What else? Who are you here with?"

"I'm here with my best friend Lilly, and a few other friends," I told him, pointing to where I'd left my friends dancing. Hopefully Lilly wasn't too eager for her drink because I could be awhile.

"What about you? Who are you here with?" I asked, curious to know everything about him.

Lucas grinned at me. "Would it sound sad if I said I was here by myself?"

"Yes, I'm afraid that would sound very sad indeed," I replied, finding I was enjoying this conversation far too much. "What's wrong with you? Don't you have any friends?"

"Actually, no, I don't. Amy, will you be my friend?" he asked, giving me a look with his blue eyes that suggested he would like to be more than friends.

My heart rate spiked and I struggled to keep up with the witty conversation that was swirling around us.

"I don't know, Lucas. You not having any friends makes me wonder if there's something wrong with you." I said this with a smile and a wink, hoping he could see that I was joking—and maybe even flirting?

He smiled widely at me, giving me a sweeping, appreciative glance that lingered on my lips.

"I've got a pretty good excuse. You see, I just moved here, am new in town and have found myself all alone," came his own flirty response.

"Hmmm, does that mean you may need a tour guide?"

His eyes flared at this as he leaned in a little closer.

"I think I'll definitely be needing a tour guide," he said in as close to a whisper as the thumping music in the club would allow. "Do you know anyone willing to do this?"

I put my hand on his arm and leaned in further, ready to offer myself up as a tour guide and more. Girlfriend or wife, perhaps? This magnetic pull I was feeling for this stranger was unlike anything I had ever felt before, and I was struggling to rein myself in.

"New from where?" I asked, working to get the conversation back on less flirty ground. And also, I was dying to place his accent.

"I just moved here from Florence, Italy."

OK, that's it, I'm dead. He was freaking foreign. And from Italy? The land of love, pasta and gelato?

"Your English is very good for someone who just arrived from Italy."

"I went to university in London and spent most of my early twenties there. I then returned home to Florence to work for a bit. And now I'm here."

"Why Melbourne?" I asked, fascinated that anyone would leave somewhere as magical-sounding as Florence to move here, but also grateful to whichever god delivered him here to me.

"It's always been on my bucket list of places to visit. Do you know Melbourne has been named the world's most liveable city for eight years in a row?"

I didn't know that and so I shook my head.

"I already love it here. There are so many cultures all crammed into this small city. It's incredible."

"I also came here for work. I start a new job on Monday," he continued, pride filling his voice. "So tonight, I'm celebrating a bit of everything. My own welcome party and..."

"And congratulations-on-your-new-job party?" I asked.

"Yes, that too," he said, his eyes making a constant trip over my face.

I felt a blush heat my face and tried to keep up with the conversation.

"So, what do you do?"

"I'm a doctor," he said, again with pride. "I start my new role as part of the trauma team at Mercy Hospital first thing on Monday morning."

At this piece of information, I froze. That couldn't be right, could *not* be my luck. This guy, this perfect man in front of me, was going to be working in my department—with me—come Monday? My body recoiled at the news and I backed away from him slowly, bumping into the person behind me, turning to apologise to them.

"Amy?" he said my name in confusion.

"I have to go! Enjoy your night."

I took in the look of concerned dismay on his face and turned to power-walk away from him. Moving at speed, like I could just feel his eyes on me asking me to come back, I made a beeline to where Lilly and Oliver were dancing.

"Lilly! We have to go!" I said, grabbing her arm and pulling her away from Oliver. As I dragged her across the dance floor, trying telepathically to impart to her the importance of leaving right now, I ordered us an Uber.

"I think I just hit on my new co-worker," I hissed at her, pulling her to get her moving faster.

"What?" Lilly asked, confused, looking back to where we'd left Oliver standing by himself.

"The new doctor, starting at the emergency department? That's him. The delicious snack over there, and I was flirting with him. We have to leave; I need to find a new job; I need to find a way to be invisible on Monday..." I continued to rant while grabbing Lilly, our coats, and running us out the door before any further damage could be done.

As we settled into the back of the car, she turned to me, bewildered. "What on earth just happened?"

"Did you see that guy I was talking to? At the bar?"

She nodded, as her eyes glazed over and her tongue hung out of her mouth.

"He's so good-looking," she told me, a dreamy look taking over her face.

"He is," I confirmed sadly. "He's also the new doctor working in the trauma team in my department, starting on Monday."

"So?" Lilly looked at me, confused.

"So, I almost kissed him. I wanted to kiss him. I wanted to do more than kiss him. And I'm going to be working with him. He doctor, me nurse," I told her with a meaningful look.

The look of comprehension on her face showed that she finally understood what was going on here.

"It doesn't always have to go the way it did the last time—" she started, before I cut her off, not wanting to go there.

"No! I'm never putting myself in that situation again," I said, working to convince myself at the same time.

We reached Lilly's apartment, where I was staying the night, and made a mad dash to her front door. Once inside, we exchanged our constrictive bar clothes for more comfortable house clothes, and settled onto Lilly's lumpy couch, when she brought up the subject again.

"Ames, you know I love you, right?"

I nodded.

"And I'll just say this once and then leave you to your own decisions. What happened with James shouldn't impact your dating life forever. The guy was a class A jerk, and what he did shouldn't colour the way you see all men in that profession."

I knew what she was saying was true, and intellectually I agreed, but I just couldn't move past it and would never put myself in that position again. I told this to Lilly, who nodded.

"OK, Ames. I support you no matter what."

"Thank you. It's all just too triggering for me. I won't go through that again."

She snuggled in close to me and rested her head on my shoulder. As I leaned my head on top of hers, she spoke up in a quiet voice, "Amy?"

"Hmm?"

"That man, Dr McHottie?" she said, giving him a *Grey's Anatomy*-adjacent nickname. Lilly loved that show. "He is so gorgeous."

I thought back to his perfectly sculpted face and had to agree. The man was beautiful.

"Yes, Dr McHottie is gorgeous. And he's so off-limits to me."

I'd said this with a finality I wasn't really feeling, determined to ignore the wave of sadness washing over me, as I reminded myself that this was how it had to be. And as I'd gone to sleep later that night, I was forced to remember, to think back to a time when a different handsome doctor had shown an interest in me. And to remember how it had all gone so horribly wrong.

I had been twenty-two years old and fresh out of university, and it was my first week at my new job. Ever since I was ten years old, I had known I wanted to be a nurse. Originally, I'd thought about becoming a doctor, but then just after my tenth birthday, my grandfather, my dear Pa, became very ill and was admitted into respite care in the local hospital. And during the many hours and days I sat with him, reading him the newspaper and watching him sleep, I had a front-row seat to the world of medicine. I watched as the doctors came and went, writing orders and briefly interacting with the patients, and then I watched the nurses. They were the lifeblood of the hospital. The ones who cared for the patients. It was the nurses who made sure Pa was comfortable in his last days, who explained all the procedures to my family, and who sat with us during his final moments. It was then that I knew exactly what I wanted to be when I grew up.

So, I worked hard to get my degree in nursing and once I graduated, I was ecstatic to be hired at the hospital of my choice, Central Melbourne Hospital, which had the number one trauma centre in the state. When I first started my degree, I'd envisioned a role in respite or aged care, given my experience with my grandfather, but then over the course of my degree, I did some shifts in the emergency room at CMH and fell in love with the fast-paced emergency department. So, getting a position there was a dream come true.

During my first week on the job, they assigned all the new nurses to work with consultants from different departments to get to know all the various specialties that rotated through the emergency room each day. I could still vividly remember the first time I saw James. He was the consultant from the cardiology department, and to me, he was perfect. Dark blonde hair, warm brown eyes. Young. He looked like an actor playing a doctor on a TV show. And he was smart, so very smart. He had an answer for everything and was always in control. Upon reflection, I could see that I was dazzled by him. By the end of the first shift working together, I had a crush on him. And looking back, I was probably pretty obvious about it. I remembered being blindsighted by the butterflies I felt just by being near him.

"So, Amy, is it?" James said, smiling his perfect white smile at me. "Are you enjoying your time here at CMH?"

I nodded, flustered that this cardio god had singled me out for some special attention.

"I am, it's great working with so many smart people," I managed to get out, blushing for no particular reason.

"Are you straight out of your degree?" he asked, walking in step with me, seeming in no hurry to end the conversation.

"Yes, I just started here on Monday."

"Well, if you need someone to show you around, just give me a buzz." And with that, he had shocked the hell out of me by grabbing my phone and programming his number into it. Then he shocked me further by calling himself from my phone. "Now I have your number too, just in case."

After that first encounter, James seemed always to be around. He would make an effort to visit me in the emergency department, even when a visit by someone from cardiology wasn't required. He started bringing me coffees and would spend his free time in the nurses' break room with me, and before the end of the month, we were texting and calling each other regularly. I was beside myself with excitement. I couldn't believe that someone as amazing as him was paying me any attention. And then after another two weeks, James had finally asked me out, and we'd become an official couple. Or so I'd thought. At the time, I had been so wrapped up in the idea of him, in the love I believed we felt for each other, that I had ignored so many signs.

"We need to keep the relationship a secret at the hospital, Ames. I don't want anyone at work thinking I'm giving my girlfriend any special treatment."

"I can't see you every weekend, Ames. To keep up with the latest research, I have to spend that time studying.

"I won't be able to introduce you to my family or friends yet, Ames. They won't understand our age difference. Let's just give it some time and then we'll reassess."

I'd been so in love with him I hadn't seen the glaring red flags being so clearly waved in front of me. Knowing that he was almost ten years older than me, I had accepted that maybe his family wouldn't be happy for him to have such a young girlfriend. And I didn't feel the need to flaunt our relationship at work, so that hadn't bothered me…too much. I had been swept up in the romance of it all. And sometimes the secrecy made things more exciting. James would grab me in the hallway and sweep me into an empty room, kiss me senseless, and then walk away. At the time, I'd thought that this was what a grown-up, passion-filled relationship was all about. I was twenty-two years old, and I didn't have a clue.

About six months after we started dating, I was at the nurses' station, having just finished a gruelling twelve-hour shift. We'd had two serious car crash victims come in earlier that day, followed by a large house fire that required all hands on deck to treat the burn patients. It was what I'd signed up for, but sometimes the aftereffects from a day like this one…it took a toll. So, at the end of this day, I was dead on my feet, eager to get home to take a shower and fall asleep. I'd been signing off on the computer when she swept into the office.

"So, you're the girl who's been screwing my husband," she said in a loud voice, drawing the attention of everyone on the floor. I turned to see a tall, thin, attractive blonde woman in the doorway. She looked to be in her early thirties. And boy, did she look angry.

I froze and looked around. Who was she talking to?

"You," she said, pointing a long finger at me. "I know you've been sleeping with my husband for the last six months. You little slut."

My face flamed with embarrassment as I noticed my friend Natalie stepping closer to me in silent support.

"I—I think you have the wrong person," I stammered. "I'm not sleeping with your husband."

"You aren't sleeping with James Martin?" she yelled, her voice getting louder with every word.

My mind screeched to a halt. James? My James? Surely, she was mistaken. I stared at the woman in front of me, whose face was red with rage, and I was briefly distracted by the screeching alarm of a code blue being called over the loudspeaker. I watched as my colleagues took off to treat this emergency call and I was drawn back to the situation in front of me. Married? James?

"Um, I'm dating James, but he isn't married. He's my boyfriend," I told her, trying to clear the air. Obviously, there had been some sort of mistake.

The lady in front of me looked at me with pity and laughed. "Your boyfriend? How can you be so stupid? He's my husband. We've been married for the last five years. We were happy until you came along," she finished, venom pouring out of her.

I looked at her, not comprehending.

"Maybe you should calm down," Natalie said in a soft voice, coming to my defence. "There's obviously been some sort of misunderstanding here. I think you can see from Amy's face she has been a victim in all of this as well."

James's wife sneered at Natalie before turning her glare back to me.

"I don't see a victim. I see a home-wrecker. And I'm asking you to stay away from my husband so we can work on mending our marriage." And with that, she stormed out of the office, leaving a trail of destruction behind her.

"Ames? Are you OK?" Natalie said, guiding me to the break room away from all the prying eyes. The remaining staff members in the office were all looking at me and whispering.

"Nat, what just happened? James is married?" I asked in disbelief. Not my James, the one who vowed to love and protect me, the man who had plans to marry me one day.

Natalie gave me a look filled with sympathy. "It would appear so, Ames. You really didn't know?"

"Know? Of course not. He pursued me. He asked me out. How could he do this to me?" As the reality of what had just transpired settled in, tears started streaming down my face.

"He's a liar and a cheat. What a dirty rat," Nat said, rubbing my back and handing me tissues.

"Oh god, Nat. I have to work here with him every day. How can I do that? And now everyone knows what I did, that I'm the 'other woman.' This is a nightmare."

Natalie had nothing to say in response, and so she just kept handing me tissues and giving me pitying looks. And I knew then that this situation was going to get worse.

And get worse, it did. In the days following my run-in with James's wife, the rumours took on a life of their own. Everywhere I went, people whispered about me. Some doctors refused to work with me. And James...well, I never heard from him again. He didn't answer a single one of my phone calls or texts. Nor did he ever provide me with any sort of explanation. He avoided working any of the same shifts as me, and whenever we needed a consult from cardiology, he sent one of his interns. This made things even worse. I was pitied, scorned and mocked. After four weeks of dealing with an untenable work environment, coupled with a broken heart and sense of trust, I started applying for other nursing roles at nearby hospitals. Lucky for me, an opening for a trauma nurse became available at Mercy Hospital and I jumped at the chance. It got even better when Natalie joined me six months later. And I never spoke another word to James or his wife again.

Following the nuclear end to this relationship, I vowed to stay away from all men. My time with James had come at a significant cost to my reputation and had almost ruined my career before it even started, the career I worked so hard to get up and running. Eventually, after some time and distance, I healed enough to amend my stance to stay away from not all men, but just men in positions of power. Men who could make my work life uncomfortable. Men who were doctors. And it was a vow I'd been determined to keep, no matter what.

And I easily kept that vow, I think as I lie here on my couch, exhausted from the memories swirling around my head. Until Lucas came along. After meeting him, I'd worked so hard to keep that vow, to keep him at arm's length, to ignore the attraction that crackled between us. And I had managed to stay away from him right until the moment when I couldn't anymore. Then it all blew up and I was left, once more, to pick up the pieces again.

I groan loudly in my silent living room, forcing myself to sit up and make my way to my bedroom, thinking about the fact that he's back in Melbourne, back in my life, and how I'll be seeing him again on Monday. Now I'm going to have to figure out how to deal with a world that contains Lucas again and find a way to survive it a second time around.

CHAPTER 3

THE MONDAY MORNING AFTER LILLY'S grand opening arrives with a large amount of trepidation on my part. I spent most of my Sunday alternating between looking for a new job—not ideal—and trying to find ways to slow down time to a complete halt. I even googled witchcraft spells, knowing full well I was acting crazy, but unable to stop myself from going over to the dark side. In my downtime, I lamented the fact that I am one of those people who doesn't have a hobby. A hobby would be so useful at times like these. It could be something I use to distract myself from my inner turmoil. The way Lilly does with her baking. I cursed myself for spending my youth reading and studying, instead of developing outside interests and becoming a more well-rounded person.

I have tried many times to find something that sticks for me. Take, for example, my living room, which is always scattered with the remnants from when I'd *last* attempted to develop a hobby. There are the bags of wool and knitting needles, one of which still has half a scarf attached to it, because I found a YouTube tutorial on how to cast on but got bored and restless and never learned how to cast off. And then there is the thousand-piece puzzle of a beautiful beach landscape, which I started with gusto and then stopped when the remaining pieces were all various shades of blue sky. Yuck. I also have a plethora of colouring books and expensive pencils, all bought around the time when adult colouring became fashionable as a way for grown-ups to de-stress. That was short-lived. And now, my current attempt at a hobby, having downloaded the "Couch to 5K" app, is learning how to run. People run for pleasure, don't they? I'm pretty sure that's what Oliver does, though he seems to do less of it now that he's with Lilly. So maybe only miserable, lonely people run for pleasure? And god knows, I'm one of them. So, running is my new hobby. I plan to start pretty soon, though, from the looks of week one on the app, it won't be easy. Five km is far, in case anyone is wondering.

I wish I could consider reading to be a hobby! Other than the knitting needles and co. taking up space, the rest of my living area is cluttered with books. Because buying a bookshelf feels like a monumental purchase, I have put it off and as such, I have collected so many I have them piled high on every surface. And while I can usually lose myself in one to escape anything negative in my life, unfortunately, my books of choice tend to fall in the romance genre, and the last thing I need in my current fragile state is to read a book about a man falling in love with a woman and then them living happily ever after. I mean, come on, guys, this just doesn't happen in real life. OK, maybe it happened for Lilly and Oliver, but they are the exception, not the rule.

So, Sunday, after updating my resume—just in case—and half-heartedly looking at a few jobs advertised online, and then finding no good time-altering spells online, I decided to forego trying to find a new book and instead, snuggled in under a blanket to reread one of my all-time favourites: *Pride and Prejudice* by Jane Austen. The perfect novel. With this book in my hot little hands, I geared myself up to devour it like I usually do, but to my dismay, I found that even the likes of Lizzie Bennet couldn't pull me out of this funk.

With this development making me even more annoyed at Lucas, who now apparently has the power to take away all my life's enjoyment, I spent some time scrolling through Instagram. After stopping at the "Love, Lilly" page and liking the thousands of photos posted from the grand opening, including the cutest one of me and Lilly together, I stumbled upon a "bookstagram" account. I then went down the rabbit hole of the Instagram book influencers—coolest job ever—and found a few who run online book clubs, choosing a book a month for everyone in the club to read and then getting together to talk about it. Now this sounded like it would be right up my alley, and some may even consider a book club a type of hobby. Spying my tattered, well-loved copy of *Pride and Prejudice* on the coffee table, I decided to start one of my own. As a way of keeping myself busy and being social, and not thinking about Lucas at all.

I pulled together a small list of friends who I thought might want to join. Sammi and Madi were an automatic invite, though I figured that Madi, with her crazy travel schedule, wouldn't commit to attend. I then added Melanie to the list, one of Lilly's new friends who'd become a staple in our friendship group in recent months, and I also included my work friend Natalie who'd just had a baby and is currently on maternity leave, so I didn't get to see her all that often. Hopefully, I'd thought, this would give her an excuse to get out of the house and meet up with friends once a month. And Lilly. That was it, that was the list. With it sorted, I sent out an email, and tucked in for the night.

TO: love.lilly@gmail.com; sammi.brown@gmail.com; madeline.russell@pharmacom.org; melanie.grace@hotmail.com; natalie.barkly@mercyhealth.com
FROM: amy.harlow@mercyhealth.com
SUBJECT: Ladies' night & book club

Hi ladies,

I have come up with the best idea! How about we start a book club? I can host it at my house, a chance for us to have a scheduled catch-up planned every month. And we can discuss a wonderful new book every month as well.

Are you guys keen?

We can start with Pride & Prejudice by Jane Austen.

I'm sure you've all read it, so it will be an easy first book to get stuck into. If you're interested, let me know and I'll send out the calendar invites.

So excited!

Always,
Amy
Xx

So, this morning as I drank my cup of coffee to cure myself of the dreaded Monday blues, I was excited to find five new emails in my inbox from my girlfriends.

TO: amy.harlow@mercyhealth.com; melanie.grace@hotmail.com; love.lilly@gmail.com; madeline.russell@pharmacom.org; natalie.barkly@mercyhealth.com

FROM: sammi.brown@gmail.com;

SUBJECT: RE: Ladies' night & book club

Amy!

A book club? Really? You need a new hobby! What happened to Couch to 5K?

I don't want to miss out on a girls' night, so count me in...

Sammi

TO: amy.harlow@mercyhealth.com; love.lilly@gmail.com; natalie.barkly@mercyhealth.com;sammi.brown@gmail.com; madeline.russell@pharmacom.org;
FROM: melanie.grace@hotmail.com;
SUBJECT: RE: Ladies' night & book club

I'm in! Thanks for including me!

Pride and Prejudice? I've never read it. Is it like a version of Bridget Jones's Diary? With Mr Darcy?

I guess I'll find out.

See you soon.
Mel

TO: amy.harlow@mercyhealth.com; love.lilly@gmail.com; melanie.grace@hotmail.com; sammi.brown@gmail.com; madeline.russell@pharmacom.org;
FROM: natalie.barkly@mercyhealth.com
SUBJECT: RE: Ladies' night & book club

Thanks, Amy. I'll try to make it.

Baby Jake is up all night at the moment teething and I'm struggling to get the basics done.

Don't think I'll have time to read the book (pretty sure I read it in high school though?!) but I'm down to catch up, if there'll be wine?

KR,
Nat

TO: amy.harlow@mercyhealth.com; sammi.brown@gmail.com; madeline.russell@pharmacom.org; melanie.grace@hotmail.com; natalie.barkly@mercyhealth.com
FROM: love.lilly@gmail.com
SUBJECT: RE: Ladies' night & book club

Pretty sure I don't have a choice. :)

I'll be there. And I will bring dessert.

Amy, there better be wine.

Love, Lilly
Xx

TO: amy.harlow@mercyhealth.com; sammi.brown@gmail.com; love.lilly@gmail.com; melanie.grace@hotmail.com; natalie.barkly@mercyhealth.com
FROM: madeline.russell@pharmacom.org;
SUBJECT: RE: Ladies' night & book club

I am currently out of the office and will reply to your email upon my return.

Madeline Russell

Excellent. My book club is off to a great start. All the girls can make it (minus Madi, who is never available for anything anymore). And while they don't appear to be overly excited by the prospect of a book club, a classic novel such as Pride and Prejudice will win them over. All those wonderful themes of love and longing in a time of different social class structures and struggles for us to explore. I can't wait. Maybe I'll put together a list of Book Club Questions, you know, to get the discussion flowing. I'm sure the girls will love that. With that sorted, I set out to gear myself up for the working week ahead, wondering what the day will bring.

I park in the spot at the hospital reserved just for nurses—spots that are a lot farther away from the entrance of the building than those reserved for the doctors, might I add. This is a constant source of annoyance amongst the nursing staff here at Mercy Hospital. It's like the class system in Pride and Prejudice, but worse. Because we should know better by now. I hold on to this extra bit of irritation and pick up my bag, filled with my packed lunch and a container of Love, Lilly cookies that she dropped over last night—that girl is the best—and head inside.

Once through the doors, I'm confronted by the daily chaos that is an emergency room in a major metropolitan hospital. There are people with bloody injuries lined up in the waiting room, with a lot of overworked and underpaid nurses tending to their needs in various ways. I look around to see whether Dr You-Know-Who has made an appearance and release a breath of relief when it looks like the coast is clear, marching to the break room to stow my bag for the day. Upon entering the room, I screech to a halt. Because there he is, studying the bulletin board—like that ever has anything interesting on it—ready to ruin my day. Lucas. As I contemplate quietly backing out of the room unseen, he speaks up.

"I know you're there, Amy. No need to run away from me like a frightened mouse."

There he is. The sarcastic man I know and—Nope, not going there.

"I wasn't going anywhere, Dr Mancini," I say to his back. He still hasn't turned around to face me. "And how did you know it was me?" I ask curiously.

Lucas turns around, his gaze running from my toes to the top of my neatly done hair, causing my heart rate to pick up.

"It's your perfume," he floors me by saying. "Distracting," he adds, under his breath.

Shocked into silence, I stare at him for a long moment. "Don't you mean overpowering? Isn't that how you once described my perfume when you asked me not to wear it to work anymore?"

Lucas looks thoughtful at this, and giving me no response, moves toward the door where I'm standing. He pauses in front of me and I hold my breath, waiting for his next move.

I watch as he reaches toward me—what's he doing?—and pulls on the door handle. As he walks around me, he says softly, "Good seeing you again, Amy. I hope you have a nice day." And then he's gone.

All the angst, hype, and dread for that? For that bland interaction with no anger or snark or anything? I look back to where he's just left and shrug my shoulders, acknowledging to myself that perhaps I've built this all up in my head, and maybe we can just work together as two grown adults. No fighting, no kissing—definitely no kissing—no anything. As I grab one of Lilly's cookies out of the container and start munching on it (I'm a self-confessed emotional eater), I ask myself why this bothers me so much. I don't want Lucas; I don't want his attention on me. So why, now that it's a reality, do I feel worse?

I stow my bag in my locker, put out the rest of the cookies on a tray and ready myself for the day ahead. After I check the board to see who I'm working with, I'm happy to find that I have the same shift as Jamie, my work bestie. Walking to the front desk, I see him already standing there, head in his hand, staring with a dreamy expression on his face into the distance. When I look at the source of his gaze, I see he's looking at Lucas and groan out loud. Jamie wasn't around last year when everything went down, and I'm not in the mood to bring him up to speed.

"Amy!" Jamie all but squeals when he sees me. "Have you seen the heavenly new doctor they hired as part of the trauma team? He's so fine my eyeballs are on fire just looking at him."

I laugh at his over-the-top dramatics. Jamie is often flamboyant and loud, but he's also the most kind-hearted person I know and the best trauma nurse I've ever worked with. The man loves to gossip and joke around, but he's also at the forefront of excellent patient care. Since Natalie left to go on maternity leave, I have called him my work best friend and occasional wingman.

"Yes, yes. I've met Dr Mancini," I tell him while sneaking a glance at Lucas myself. He's still so good-looking. Damn it. "And yes, he's very nice to look at and all that, but can we please get to work?"

Jamie continues to stare at Lucas, fanning himself theatrically.

"I don't think I'll be capable of working with that man in my vicinity. Do we know if he's straight?"

Can I mess with Lucas here a little by indulging Jamie's interest? I think. No, that wouldn't be a nice thing to do to my friend, but boy, it would be fun watching Lucas try to get away from a very determined loved-up Jamie.

"Yes, he's straight," I tell him instead, going to wash my hands to ready myself for the start of my shift.

"A shame." Jamie pouts, brightening suddenly when he looks at me. "A shame for me, but girl, you should so hit that."

I shake my head with a little laugh and tell him, "My friend, you don't know what you're saying. We need a therapy session based around that man someday soon."

His eyes light up at the thought of juicy gossip, however as he goes to probe for more information, a trauma comes through the doors, throwing us into work mode. We both turn to see two stretchers being wheeled in by the paramedics, both with bloody patients on them. One patient is groaning loudly; the other is deadly silent. Jamie looks at me and we snap into motion, knowing that a silent patient is a critical patient. As we rush to gather the equipment necessary for what looks like a code blue, Jamie turns to me with raised eyebrows.

"You owe me details," he hisses as we make our way toward the stretchers.

"Put aside some time, Jamie. This story is a doozy."

CHAPTER 4

LATER THAT NIGHT, AFTER A busy and stressful shift with a high number of cardiac arrest patients, Jamie and I make our way to the local bar, the one where all the hospital staff congregate after a difficult day to unwind and debrief before heading home. This place is popular because it's close to the hospital and it serves cheap alcohol. I haven't told Lilly about it, because she already thinks I work in *Grey's Anatomy* and I don't want to feed into the fantasy by adding the element of Joe's Bar into the mix. After Jamie and I have placed our order for drinks and some food to nibble on, he turns to me and demands I tell him everything.

I start by detailing the first meeting with Lucas that night at the bar for Lilly's birthday, watching in amusement as the story continues and his eyes grow wider. "And then what happened? What happened when you went to work that following Monday?" he asks, watching me with bated breath.

I sigh and take a sip of my drink, letting my mind drift back to that first day in the hospital with Lucas, and everything that followed it.

That Monday morning two years ago, following my first encounter with Lucas at the bar, I had been filled with dread as I dressed for work. I couldn't believe that the hot doctor I'd just met was going to be working in the same hospital as me. In an attempt to look as different from "bar Amy" as possible, I had put my hair back in a severe braid and used a light touch when doing my makeup. In my scrubs, with the harsh fluorescent lights of the emergency room washing all the colour out of me, I hoped to look unrecognisable to Lucas.

As we gathered for the weekly staff meeting, I found a chair in the back and tried to hide behind some of the taller members of the group. I kept my head down, appearing to be busy scrolling on my phone when Natalie, my friend and colleague, plonked down next to me with a sigh.

"Why are we sitting all the way back here?" she asked, her eyebrows pulled down in a puzzled frown. We both usually sat up the front, closer to the donuts and coffee.

"Ummm," I replied, trying to buy some time to come up with a viable excuse. "Just mixing things up, keeping things fresh."

Natalie gave me an even more confused look at this bizarre response and started to follow up when Hector, the head of emergency medicine, cleared his throat to gain everyone's attention. As the meeting started, I looked around me and felt a sense of relief. No Lucas in sight. Maybe he had the name of the hospital mixed up? Though that was unlikely, given there were no other hospitals with a name similar to ours. As I was pondering this, my attention was brought back to what Hector was saying.

"And I'd like to introduce you all to the new member of our trauma unit, Dr Lucas Mancini. Joining us from the Santa Maria Hospital in Florence, Italy, Dr Mancini completed his medical degree at the University of London, where he specialised in Emergency Medicine. He will bring to the team many years of expertise in this area, and I know you will all make him feel welcome."

Hector continued to drone on with his little speech, but the blood rushing to my ears drowned him out. Lucas was here. And just as the realisation sunk in that I would be working with him after all, I felt a rush of awareness race down my spine. I knew this feeling; it was the same one I'd felt at the bar when Lucas had stood behind me. With a feeling of resignation at what I knew I would find, I turned slowly to see him sitting in the chair behind me, his head tilted in shocked recognition as he stared straight back at me. There he was. In the flesh. *In his beautiful flesh,* my dirty mind amended.

"Dr Mancini, would you like to say a quick word to the team?" Hector's voice interrupted our staring session.

I blushed as Lucas continued to stare at me, seeming not to have heard his name being called. Embarrassed now, aware the entire team was staring at us staring at each other, I wrenched my eyes away from his and forced myself to face the front.

"Dr Mancini? Lucas?" Hector tried again.

"Right, sorry! I must still be in the Italian time zone," Lucas said, his joke and his accent instantly charming the crowd.

I watched as he unfolded his large frame from the uncomfortable fold-out chair and walked with confidence to the front of the room. This was a man who felt at home being in charge.

"*Buongiorno*," he began, causing every female in the room to sigh. "I am thrilled to be here with you all today and to join such an accomplished team. I hope to learn the ways of working from each of you and I hope together we can make this department run more smoothly."

More smoothly? I thought in a huff. *Who does this guy think he is? Coming in here all new and shiny, thinking he knows better?* I looked around to see if any of my co-workers were taking similar offence to what this guy was saying, only to be confronted by a group of people who appeared to be eating right out of his hands.

"I know that there are ways of doing things. That is how they have always been done. But I hope you will be open to changing things and making them better," he continued, making my blood boil further. He had been here all of two minutes. How could he possibly know if something needed to be changed to be better?

I watched as my traitorous colleagues all nodded along, noting that the women in particular seemed keen to be involved in whatever Dr Mancini was proposing. As I turned to Natalie to roll my eyes at her, ensuring that we were on the same anti-change, anti-Lucas page, I saw she was sitting forward in her seat, her cheeks flushed, eyes glued to the man at the front of the room. Natalie "happily married" Barkly. Great, it appeared I had lost her too.

"So, after I have settled in, I hope I can meet with each of you, one-on-one," he said, zeroing his eyes in on me. I sunk into my seat and looked at the floor. "And I hope we will all have a harmonious working relationship moving forward." He finished up to a spontaneous round of applause, like he had given us the answer to solving world peace or something, for goodness' sake.

After the meeting was over, I sprinted out of the room, ignoring the alarmed faces as I rush through the crowd, all of whom seemed eager to hang around and meet the new doctor in town. I had no such inclination; my sole focus was to put as much distance between myself and Lucas as possible. And I knew this was only a temporary reprieve, given that we had to work near each other, but right now, every minute and every metre away from him felt imperative to my sense of equilibrium.

Once I had safely locked myself in the women's toilets, I put my back against the wall and allowed myself to sink to the floor. I took a deep breath in and acknowledged that the way I was acting was a little extreme. So, we met at a bar, we flirted for a few minutes. And what? It's not like we crossed any lines. Why was I getting so worked up? And why was the thought of him being here and wanting to change things making me feel so antsy? I rested my head against the wall and tried to get myself together. *There is nothing here that I cannot manage,* I told myself in a reasonable internal voice. He was just another person who I had to work with. I worked with lots of people every day. He was just another one of those. A nobody, really. I nodded my head at this last thought. Yes, a nobody. And with this in mind, I pulled myself up, fixed my fly-away hairs in the mirror, took a deep breath and opened the door to start the day—

"Oooof!" And walked straight bang into Dr Lucas McHottie Mancini.

"Amy," he said in that deep voice of his, grabbing my arm to steady me. His subtle accent doing all the things to my insides.

"Good morning, Dr Mancini," I said, proud that my voice was not as wobbly as my knees, pulling my arm away from his and stepping back to give myself some space.

Lucas ran his hand through his hair, looking a lot less composed than he did earlier.

"You work here?" he asked, sounding incredulous.

I nodded as I looked around, trying to find a polite but speedy way out of this situation.

"I do," I confirmed, spying Natalie across the room and waving at her.

She gave me a strange look and waved back.

"I have to go, my colleague needs me," I say, pointing to where Natalie was still giving me a bemused half-wave.

Lucas continued to stare at me, shaking his head in amazement, and then he stepped to the side.

"I look forward to our meeting, Amy. I've asked Hector to schedule ours for first thing tomorrow morning. Until then," he said, turning my world upside down and walking away.

Tomorrow morning? I thought as I walked over to a curious-looking Natalie. Great, I could kiss the notion of sleeping tonight goodbye.

The next morning, after a terrible night's sleep and an inordinate amount of procrastinating, I steeled myself and knocked on the door of Lucas's office. Because of course Dr Fancy Pants got an office.

"Come in," he said, his voice sending a shiver down my spine, even through a solid wooden door.

I entered the room, leaving the door wide open to avoid any appearance of intimacy, and took a seat in front of him.

"Good morning, Dr Mancini," I said, using his title as a way of keeping things formal between us.

Lucas narrowed his eyes in a way that let me know he was on to me and my petty attempt at keeping my distance. "Good morning, Amy."

"I prefer that doctors here address me as Nurse Harlow," I told him in a low voice.

"Hiya, Ames," came the voice of Dr Rydell, one of the junior consultants and now an ex-friend of mine, as he walked by the doorway.

Lucas raised an eyebrow at me, silently calling me a little liar, and I felt myself blush right up to my ear tips. This had not gotten off to a good start.

"As I was saying, *Amy*," he continued, while I contemplated ways of disappearing into the floor. "I wanted to clear the air with you. About that night."

I gave him my "practised all night in the mirror" confused look and asked, "What night?"

Lucas sighed with a hint of impatience. "You know what night I am referring to? It was three days ago. At Bar Phoenix?" he added when I continued to give him a blank look.

"Oh yes, that's right, Bar Phoenix."

"Yes, well, I want to make my intentions apparent right off the bat—"

I cut him off before he could go any further, not wanting to know the end of that sentence, because either scenario was bad for me. If his intention was to put it behind us, well, that was just asking for an awkward rejection conversation, and any plans to continue the flirtation were now a moot point. So, I got in first. "I'm not sure where you're going with this, but either way, it's unnecessary," I said with a firm nod of my head.

"Amy, we had a moment at that bar."

I ignored the thrill of this statement and ploughed on. "I had many conversations at the bar, spoke to many men that night—" I stopped short as his eyes grew heated.

"So, I'm one of many men you flirted with that night?" he asked, an edge to his voice.

Hmmm, I seemed to have put myself into a bit of a pickle here. Admit that I spoke to many men and I sound like the sort of woman I wasn't, or else admit that the moment with him was an anomaly. One that I could not stop thinking about. I went with the former.

"Yes, I spoke to many *people* that night. You and I had a nice little chat, not much more to say about it," I said, lying through my teeth.

Lucas stared at me, and then sighed again, this time with what looked like disappointment.

"OK. Let's play it your way. I just wanted to make sure we can work together without you feeling uncomfortable around me."

"Full comfort here." Shut up, Amy!

"Great, because Hector and I have decided that the emergency department needs a bit of a shake-up. And I've nominated you as the point person for the nurses. So, you and I will be working closely together for the next several months."

At this, all thoughts of flirtation and "moments" flew out of my head. *Here he goes again with wanting to change things in this place where things are already working just fine.*

"Perhaps you should try working in a place for more than a day before you decide it needs to be changed," I said through gritted teeth, surprising us both with my anger.

"You think I'm too quick to make a judgement? Are you doubting my abilities before you even know what they are?"

"Isn't that what you're doing with the department? Doubting that it runs well before you've even had time to work it?"

We stared at each other, neither one wanting to concede an inch and just as I was about to cave and speak first, he said, "Well, how about you show me how it all works. I will shadow you for the next few days and you can convince me that nothing needs to be changed."

Shadow me? As in, be my shadow? I thought in a panic.

"Is that really necessary?" I asked in desperation.

"You seem to think it is. And I agree with you, I need to get to know the place and what better way than through the eyes of someone who works here. I'll speak to Hector about shadowing you for the next...week?" he asked, almost to himself. "Yes, a week should be enough time. I'm not officially on the roster until next Monday, anyway. So, I'll be at your side night and day until then."

Lucas gave me a triumphant smile, and I knew he had outplayed me.

"I see you are working the morning shift tomorrow, Nurse Harlow. I'll be here bright and early to accompany you through your day."

As he finished this, his victory speech, he'd gotten up and motioned me out the door. Numbly, I complied, walking out of his office, cursing him with every bad word I knew in my mind.

"See you soon," had been his parting words.

I'd said nothing. I knew what I had done. In trying to win the battle of our wills, I had accidentally lost the war. The war being to stay away from Lucas. And boy, had I lost it big time.

I finish detailing these encounters with Lucas as I rip the label from my long-forgotten beer. Jamie sits frozen in front of me, eyes wide as saucers and glowing with excitement with every juicy nugget I share. What can I say? The man loves drama.

"So then what happened? Please tell me there was a whole heap of fighting that led to a whole heap of lovemaking?"

I blush and laugh. "Well, you got the fighting part right. We were at war from that day onward. We couldn't find one single thing to agree on."

"But there must have been more?" he says.

"There was," I reply with a deep sigh. "A lot more. But that's a story for another time."

Jamie looks like he wants to probe for more details, but he must see something in my face to make him change his mind.

"So, what does that mean for now? Now that he's back. How are the two of you going to work together?"

"That's the million-dollar question, Jamie," I say with a grimace. "I actually have no idea."

CHAPTER 5

As it turns out, I had no reason to be concerned. In complete contrast to what I thought was going to be a working environment fraught with tension and awkwardness, was actually a working relationship filled with...nothing. And in the weeks following Lucas's return from Florence, we seemed to have settled into a routine, one where I avoid being around him, and he appears to be fine with it. There are no Monday morning unplanned one-on-one meetings, no roster changes where we end up on the same shift together every day, no epic fights in the break room. Nothing. And it's messing with my head. It's weird to think that he hasn't tried to explain to me what happened last year, when he left so abruptly. He doesn't appear to be apologetic or remorseful, and it's so strange considering he is the bad guy in the situation. Instead, he's just there, another face in the crowd. And I know it should please me that things are not awkward at work, but I feel quite the opposite. I didn't want things to be uncomfortable, but I also didn't want to feel invisible, either.

"Isn't this what you wanted?" Lilly asks, as we FaceTime each other on Friday night and I fill her in on the events of another long week of Lucas's apathy.

"I guess? I don't know. Maybe I wanted an apology? An explanation? Something?"

"But did you actually want that?" Lilly says. "You haven't been open to hearing his apology or even an explanation. You were quick to shut him down at my grand opening."

"You're right," I say, before continuing. "It's just so confusing. I can't figure out what I want from him, if I want anything at all." I finish my little speech with a pout that I just can't hold in.

"That's natural. At a minimum, he should apologise for what he did. The jerk!" Lilly says, angry all over again on my behalf.

"Yes, that's right, he's a jerk! And we've talked about him enough! Now tell me, have you read *Pride and Prejudice* for next week's book club?"

She gives me a sheepish look and holds up the DVD of the movie adaptation.

"Don't hate me Ames, I just don't have time to read it. But I promise to watch the movie, so I can at least contribute to the discussion," she says, holding up a printed list of the book club questions I sent out to the group. "And I'll also bring brownies and cookies to make up for being so slack!"

I feel bad for putting pressure on my friends to complete "homework," so I rush to reassure her, "It's fine, Lil. Just watch the movie if you have time. That version is excellent. I love it! And don't worry about the questions, I only put them together to help with the discussion." Feeling lame, I finish, "It's not mandatory."

Lilly laughs. "I know, and I know you won't be giving out detentions to those who don't complete the required reading. I just want to make sure I can take part with you guys, and I know how much you love this book."

It's true. I really love this book.

"Oh hey," she says, changing the subject. "I know what will cheer you up after a long week at the hospital!"

"What?"

"Let's go to the dog shelter tomorrow, the one down near the Market Place...Paws R' Us? We can play with some puppies, maybe help for the day? They always need people to take the dogs for walks or help with grooming and stuff."

"That sounds like a perfect way to spend the day," I tell her, excited by the thought. "But...are you sure you'll be able to do this and not want to take them all home with you? You know Oliver hasn't exactly warmed to the idea of you guys getting a dog."

Now it's Lilly's turn to pout at this reminder, but then her face brightens. "I'm sure it will be fine. Just play with some puppies and leave. No problem at all."

I look at the dreamy expression on her face and can almost guarantee she'll leave the shelter tomorrow with a dog under her arm. And as I picture the look on Oliver's face when he sees Lilly return home with what is bound to be the most chaotic dog ever, it's making me want to be involved even more.

"OK, let's do it!"

We hang up the call and I spend the rest of the evening attempting to think only about puppies. And not about Lucas. Except my brain isn't co-operating with me and right before I'm about to fall asleep, thoughts of him fill my mind. And I'm struck by one specific memory, a memory I've worked so hard to suppress. The memory of *that* night, the one where Lucas finally went from being my enemy to something so much more.

It was one year ago, a whole year after Lucas and I first met, on the night of Lilly's twenty-fourth birthday, and once again I'd had to drag the poor heartbroken girl out to celebrate her birthday. She'd had such little luck around this time of year, but hopefully this time would be different. I'd sent Oliver a few texts to tell him to get himself into gear and I just needed to make sure she didn't leave the bar before he got here. Just as I was thinking this, I heard the music change to Perfect by Ed Sheeran, and I knew Oliver had taken my advice to heart and that he wouldn't screw this up. I watched as Lilly floated toward where he was standing waiting for her, a look of adoration on his face, and I was confident that this would be the night that they'd finally get their act together.

"Do you think they'll finally get their act together?" Madi asked as we watched, our eyes glued to the show unfolding in front of us.

"I think they will." Ever the romantic, Sammi appeared next to us and was watching them with heart shapes in her eyes.

"Yes, it's their time. No more miscommunication. They're meant to be together," I stated with pure confidence. I had been watching the two of them pine over each other in secret for long enough.

"Who's meant to be together?" came a voice from behind me.

Madi and Sammi both stared at the owner of the voice behind me and from the dazed looks on their faces, I knew it could only be one person.

"Dr Mancini," I said, turning to look at him with my eyebrows raised. "Are you stalking me?"

I ran my eyes over Lucas as he stood in front of me, taking in his "night out at a bar" attire. Blue jeans, fitted nice and snug, and a black button-down shirt rolled up to display his sexy forearms—

who knew forearms could be so sexy?—he looked just like a Calvin Klein model. And thinking of him as a Calvin Klein model made me wonder what he looked like in just a pair of Calvin Klein underwear, and—stop it, Amy! He's your nemesis. Pull yourself together.

"No stalking, just a night out with my friends," he said, pulling me out of my inappropriate thoughts and pointing to a group of men all lounging at the bar, staring at us with interest. "I saw you over here, thought it would be the polite thing to come say hi."

"Polite?" I said in a tart voice. "You know what that is?"

"Well, English isn't even my first language, but believe me, I know the meaning of polite a lot better than you."

How dare he! I thought.

"Oh really? Was it polite of you to change all of my day shifts last week to night shifts?"

"Was it polite for you to roster only student nurses in my service for the last month? So that I basically spent every day with a bumbling fool following me around?" he threw back at me, without missing a beat.

I smiled at this reminder. That one had been clever, as it wasn't obvious to anyone but me. And Lucas.

"I don't know what you're talking about. It just worked out that way." I looked at him, widening my eyes to show my innocence.

Lucas laughed at this, flashing his brilliant, blinding smile at me. It really wasn't fair that his smile made my insides quiver. Every single time.

"You're a pain in my arse, Harlow," he said, drawing my attention to his perfectly sculpted arse. Hmm, it was a good one.

I looked back to find Madi and Sammi watching this exchange with glee, their heads going back and forth between us, like they were watching a tennis match.

"Ahem, Amy? Are you going to introduce us?" Sammi asked, her eyes alight with mischief.

"Lucas, these are my friends Madi and Sammi. Girls, this is Lucas. Otherwise known as Lucifer himself."

The devil in question laughed loudly at this while he leaned forward to shake their hands.

"It's a pleasure to meet you both. Any friend of Amy's is a friend of mine."

I heard the sarcasm in this statement, while my so-called friends lapped it up. They were enamoured with him. Even after everything I'd told them, one flash of his pretty blue eyes and his pearly white smile and they were a puddle of feminine adoration. It happened every time.

"Can I get you ladies a drink?" Lucas asked, continuing to win them over. The jerk.

"No, how about we get this round," Madi replied, pulling on Sammi's arm and dragging her away from her unabashed appraisal of Lucas. "We'll be back soon. Try not to kill each other while we're gone."

I shot daggers at the two of them as they skipped away. Sammi actually had the nerve to turn around and blow me a kiss as she went. I needed new friends.

"So, what are we watching?" Lucas asked, resting his elbows on the table in front of us, making himself at home.

I sighed, knowing he wouldn't be leaving me alone. "That's Lilly over there," I told him, pointing to where she and Oliver were in an intense discussion. "And that fool with her is my brother. I'm hoping he's currently grovelling for her forgiveness after royally screwing up last week."

Lucas focused back on me, giving me his undivided attention. "What'd he do?"

"He was a typical man. When the time came to stand up and declare his feelings for Lilly—feelings he's had for years—he chickened out and hurt her in the process. Men! You're all so emotionally stunted."

His eyes lit up at this. "You don't have a very generous perception of our fair sex, do you?"

"In my experience, you guys tend to be more trouble than you're worth."

He started to say something at this, but I shushed him as I watched Lilly and Oliver kissing. And kissing some more. OK gross, he *was* my brother after all.

"They're kissing!" Madi squealed, popping up next to me, two drinks in hand.

"Finally!" Sammi echoed, handing a drink to Lucas.

We watched as Lilly and Oliver came up for air and shoot a look over at us. I blew her a kiss, only just resisting the urge to jump up and down with excitement. I was so happy for them.

"You look happy," Lucas whispered, his lips close to my ear.

I tried to ignore the goose bumps that were travelling down my body and turned my head to his. Big mistake. Lucas's face was close to mine, his blue eyes staring into my eyes. Gulp. I wanted to kiss him. No, Amy! Down girl! He's not the person you should be kissing.

"I am," I said, cursing the fact that my voice was coming out all breathy.

He took this as an invitation to look at my lips, his eyes darkening with longing.

"Abort!" I yelled, out loud. Dammit, I was meant to think that, not say it!

Lucas straightened up with a grin and didn't call me out on my craziness, for once letting me off the hook.

"Ames, we're leaving now," Madi says, drawing my attention away from the man in front of me.

I looked to where my friends were gathering up their bags and coats and went to collect my things as well.

"You're leaving?" Lucas said from beside me, looking...disappointed? No, that couldn't be right.

"Yes, we all came together, so they're my lift home..." I trailed off, not sure where my thoughts were. I didn't want to stay here with Lucas, did I?

"Would you be interested in—" he stopped, looking uncertain. So unlike his normal, confident self.

"Interested in...?" I asked, a bit too eagerly.

He gave me a half smile at this. "Interested in going to get some food?" he asked, looking at his watch. "Perhaps a midnight snack? With me?"

It shocked me how much I wanted to. What spell had he cast over me in this bar tonight?

"OK," my mouth squeaked, before my brain could talk it out of it.

"'OK'?" Lucas's face brightened with a big smile, like I had given him a gift. Oh boy, I was in trouble with this one.

"Right, Ames. You go with Lucas and we'll make our way home. Let's go say goodbye to the lovebirds over there," Sammi summarised, effectively squashing any way for me to get out of my impromptu midnight snack with Lucas.

The three of us charged over to the happy couple, giving them big hugs and many warnings to Oliver not to mess up again. Like seriously, if he did, I'd disown him.

"We're leaving now," I told the loved-up Lilly, who was glowing with the happiness she was so clearly feeling. "Happy birthday!"

"Thank you, Ames. We couldn't have done this without you."

I walked back to where Lucas was waiting for me, feeling a sense of pride at the love match well-made, and took a deep breath. What did the night ahead hold for me?

Lucas and I had found an all-night cafe, not too far away from the bar. It served pancakes and French fries, so I was sold.

"Really, Ames? Pancakes and fries?" Lucas asked, his eyebrows raised in surprise, causing my heart to skip a beat at the use of my nickname. He'd never called me that before.

"But of course. Name a better combination, I dare you," I responded, trying to ignore the way being with him and not fighting was making me feel.

"Um, how about pasta and wine? Or pizza and wine? Or antipasti and wine?" he said, his Italian accent making his suggestions sound all the more appealing.

"So, basically anything with wine? Is that the Italian way?"

"Better than whatever this is," he said, as the mountain of food arrived in front of me.

"Don't knock it till you try it." I dipped a piece of my pancake in maple syrup and added a fry to the fork. "Here, give it a go. I dare you!"

He crinkled his nose as he appraised the offering in front of him. Looking at me, then the food, then back to me—my lips, to be specific—he opened his mouth for me to feed him. And the temperature had suddenly gone up in the restaurant. *Is the heater broken?* I thought, feeling sweat drip down my back. Gross.

As my face heated, I popped the food into his mouth, scooting back to my side of the table and fanning myself with my napkin. Something was definitely wrong with the heat in this place.

"Ok, you're right," he said, chewing his food with a thoughtful expression on his face. "This combination totally works. Sweet and savoury in just the right amounts."

"Right?" I said, pleased that we could finally agree on something, while shovelling a forkful of pancake into my mouth.

"Right," his voice was soft as he reached over to wipe some syrup off my lips.

My brain froze at the intimacy of the gesture, while my treacherous body took over, turning my lips into the palm of his hand, silently asking for more. It was like my lips had a mind of their own tonight.

Lucas's eyes darkened at this, and he leant forward.

"I'm going to kiss you now," he said, pausing to give me a chance to reject him.

"OK." My voice sounded unfamiliar to me, all breathless and sexy.

Then he was there, moving in slow motion, getting closer and closer and—

"Can I get you kids anything else?" the hundred-year-old waitress asked, choosing this moment to become a beacon of customer service.

"No!" I yelled out loud. Protesting the interruption and telling her to go away in one word.

Lucas chuckled at my response, leaning back and smiling at Betty, the waitress.

"What my friend here means is that we are fine, thank you. Maybe we'll just get the bill?" he said, charming his way out of the situation.

"You got it, handsome." She winked at him, throwing me a dirty look as she walked away. Fair.

Lucas looked at me, seeming uncertain again. "So, what now?"

"Now?" I repeated, thinking about our almost kiss and feeling brave and reckless in equal measure. "Now I think I want to see where you live."

As soon as these words were out of my mouth, my mind-of-its-own mouth, he was up and out of his seat. He threw a stack of cash on the table and grabbed my hand, yanking me out of my seat. Like he was scared if he waited even a minute, I would change my mind.

"Slow down, Lucas," I said, feeling empowered by his obvious enthusiasm at my request. "I'm not going anywhere."

"You're not?" he asked, his voice husky. "Because I've waited for this for a long time."

The sincerity in his voice stopped me from teasing him for his display of vulnerability.

After we had left the café and were heading to his car, I decided to reward him with some honesty of my own.

"I've wanted you for a long time, too."

He stopped at my declaration then and pulled me into his arms.

"So, you don't hate me after all?"

"I wouldn't say that," I said back, unable to resist a bit of teasing.

Lucas smiled his special smile at this and pulled me in closer. Kissing my forehead and causing a flurry of butterflies to take off in my stomach, he moved down to give me a gentle Eskimo kiss.

The sensation of his nose rubbing gently against mine made my knees weak, and I knew I needed more. And I needed it now.

"Let's go to your place," I whispered in his ear, kissing his neck, eliciting a soft moan from him. Hmm, a sensitive spot. I kissed him there again, this time getting a grunt in return. In an instant, he'd picked me up and was spinning me around, racing to his car. When we got there, he put me down gently, both of us laughing and breathless.

"Are you sure you want to do this?" he asked, one last time. I hoped.

Suddenly, I was beyond sick of all the talking, we had spent so much time talking. I reached up and pulled his lips down to mine. And I kissed him. After the initial touch of his lips on mine, Lucas took over, weaving his hands into my hair and deepening the kiss. I sunk into it and opened my mouth, tentatively touching his tongue with my own, eliciting another moan from him, this one louder and filled with need.

"Let's go," he breathed out, lifting his head from mine and reaching behind him to open my car door.

As I went to step into the car, he grabbed my hand and stopped me. Bending down, seeming unable to resist, he gave me one more kiss. A gentle pressing of his lips to mine, tasting me, and I sighed all the way down to my toes.

"Let's go," I parroted back to him when he released my lips. It was now imperative that we get to his place. As. Soon. As. Possible.

I sat down in the passenger seat, allowing Lucas to reach over and do up my seat belt—sigh—not letting myself stop and think about what we'd just done, and what we were about to do. Fully acknowledging that this night had been many months in the making. Every passionate argument, every angry word, every heated glance had all led us to this.

"Ready?" Lucas asked, putting the car into gear and giving me a small smile.

"Yes," I answered, with a firm nod.

I knew a part of me had been ready for this moment for almost a year. And there was no turning back now.

The next morning, I woke up feeling utterly content. I stretched, feeling sore in the most delicious way, and reached for Lucas. Only to find that he wasn't there, snuggled up next to me, where I'd left him. Gingerly, I opened one of my eyes, which had wanted to stay shut during what I had hoped would be a morning cuddle session and found Lucas on the phone pacing around the room.

"*Rallenta e dimmi coas e successo?*" he fired off in rapid Italian, his voice filled with urgency.

Watching his face grow more concerned as he listened to whoever was on the other end of the line, I immediately sat up and started to search around for my clothes.

Lucas, hearing me, looked up and frowned. He glanced away and walked out of the room, still speaking in Italian.

"What's *that* all about?" I muttered to myself, standing up and getting dressed, the need to not be naked in Lucas's bed suddenly overwhelming me.

"Sorry about that," he said as he reentered the room, his face preoccupied.

"Is everything OK?" I asked, concerned for him.

"I'm not sure." He was walking around, grabbing things and throwing them on the bed. I looked at him closely as he walked past me. His jaw was clenched and his hands kept making a constant trip through his hair. He looked rattled.

"Hey?" I said, trying to get back the Lucas from the night before. "Tell me what's happening."

"I'm sorry," he said, looking at me finally, his face full of something…? Regret? "I need you to leave. It's nothing to do with you. I just need to focus on something at the moment."

I felt the breath leave me at this. He needed me to leave? What was going on?

"You want me to go?" I asked, my voice small and shaky.

Lucas came over to me and took my hands. Better, but still not great, I thought.

"I just have an emergency and I need to leave. You can stay if you want? Make yourself some breakfast…?" He trailed off, walking to his closet to get god knew what. His whole demeanour had changed from the man I was familiar with. He seemed frazzled, a stressed-out energy rolling off him as he appeared to be processing that phone call.

"An emergency?" I tried again. "Anything I can help with?"

"Not really," came his answer from inside his closet. "I'll call you when I know more."

I thought about the conversation I'd overheard, one that I couldn't understand, but that was fraught with something, and I let it go. I decided to give him some space to deal with whatever it was, and then let him come back to me.

"We're both on the same shift at the hospital tonight," I told his back as he walked away toward the bathroom. "We can talk then."

"Ahh, sure. We'll talk later," came his muffled reply as he darted from room to room, somewhat frantically.

"OK, well, bye."

With only silence answering me, I ordered myself an Uber and let myself out of the building. As I sat on the kerbside waiting for my ride home, I tried not to read into what had happened. *I'll see Lucas later this afternoon, and we'll clear this all up*, I thought, trying not to cry. And as I reminisced about the night we had just spent together, I convinced myself that this could not possibly be the way things ended for us.

With this thought, I talked myself into a better place and by the time I arrived at the hospital later that day I was feeling hopeful that things would turn out OK. But then, instead of seeing Lucas and clearing the air as I had hoped, the first person I saw was Hector. Who promptly told me that Lucas had left to return home to his *girlfriend* in Florence. It was history repeating itself. Every fear I'd ever had about entering a relationship with Lucas had come back to the surface and I was bombarded by images of James's wife yelling at me and calling me the 'other woman.' I'd done it again! The shock and the pain of this betrayal coming after the incredible night we'd just shared had me shutting down, and without thinking, I'd picked up my phone and did the only thing left in my control. I blocked him. Everywhere. My phone, email, social media. And in doing this, I'd attempted to erase him from my mind and my heart. Completely.

With a start, I wake up back in the here and now, memories of that moment with Hector reverberating through my brain. I roll over in bed and wipe the tears off my cheeks, cursing myself for thinking about Lucas instead of puppies like I should have been. With a sigh, I look at the clock and calculate how many hours I have left before I can get up and spend the day with Lilly, a day where I can distract myself from thinking about the man who I'd tried so hard not to let into my heart. And who had broken it all the same.

CHAPTER 6

THE NEXT MORNING, AFTER I'VE consumed several cups of coffee to compensate for my restless night's sleep, I open the door for Lilly who arrives armed with banana bread, straight from the oven, and big news.

"We've picked a date for the wedding," she says, as I open the door to let her in.

"You have? When is it?" I ask, ushering her in and taking the tasty treat from her. It's still warm and just the smell of it is making my mouth water. We set our little feast of banana bread and freshly brewed coffee on my kitchen table and Lilly launches into planning mode.

"We took so long to get together, we don't want to wait to get married. So we're looking at a June winter wedding."

"June? That's only a few months from now!" I exclaim in surprise.

"I know. But Oliver is good at planning, so I know it'll be fine. He's in charge of the venue, guest list, menu, music, photographer and the honeymoon."

"And what have you got on your list?"

She counts off her fingers as she lists, "My dress, the dessert and cake, and picking my maid of honour. That's you, by the way. So, yay! One thing off my list." She finishes with a big smile.

Tears fill my eyes as I look at her, my almost-sister-in-law to be. "It would be my honour to be your maid of honour, Lil. I promise to do everything I can to ensure your wedding day is the best ever."

Lilly leans over and envelops me in a bear hug as we both let out a few tears.

"Now we've settled this, you also have the privilege of planning my bachelorette party."

"Oh, I'm so all over that!" I tell her, filled with excitement at the thought. "It's going to be epic."

"Good, I know it's in safe hands. Now let's play with some puppies!"

When we arrive at the local puppy shelter, Paws R' Us, I know without a doubt that Lilly will adopt a dog today. There's no way we are leaving here, just the two of us.

"Oooh, look at them all," Lilly squeals, kneeling down on the floor and letting a bunch of them jump all over her. "They're so cute!"

I watch as she sits down and starts patting them one at a time, letting them jump up to lick her face and then lying down on the floor and wrestling with them. She's in doggie heaven.

"They're so sweet, Ames," she says, looking up at me, her face shining with happiness. Lilly has always had the most expressive face, and for the last year, since she and Oliver got together, she's been radiating joy.

"They are," I tell her, sitting down next to her and promptly getting bombarded with furry bodies.

We spend the next hour playing with, feeding, and grooming a group of rescue dogs, all there waiting for someone to adopt them and take them to their forever home. And by the end of that hour, I'm with Lilly, ready to take them all home with me.

"Have you noticed that little guy over there?" Lilly asks me now, pointing to a chocolate-coloured dog in the corner. He looks like a small teddy bear and he hasn't come near us all day.

"Yeah, he seems timid."

We both take him in as he sits in the corner, watching us with wary eyes, shaking slightly.

"All the other dogs have come over to say hello, but that little guy seems to be scared," she says, her eyes sad.

"That's Frank," one of the regular shelter volunteers pipes up. "He's scared of his own shadow. We don't know his story, but he doesn't interact with us like the rest of the pack. He's a Spoodle, that's a Poodle mixed with a Cocker Spaniel," he clarifies when we look at him with confusion. "And that breed is normally very friendly. Franky over there isn't like that at all. He's just a little bundle of nerves, poor thing."

Lilly thinks about this as she watches Frank and then gets up to walk over to him, ever so slowly. She stops a few steps from him and says in a low voice, "Hey there, little man, I'm Lilly."

Frank stops shaking and looks at her, his head tipped to the side like he's contemplating her, before moving closer. Lilly reaches her hand out for him to sniff and smiles big when he licks it.

With a giggle, she picks him up, and he nuzzles into her arms and I watch as they fall in love. In that moment, I know that any hopes Oliver had for a puppy-free house have disappeared.

"He's mine," she says, turning around to me with Frank in her arms. She's beaming. "Isn't he the cutest dog you've ever seen?"

I have to admit that Frank is adorable and the two of them together make quite the picture, but I decide to be the voice of reason.

"Lilly, you promised Oliver that you wouldn't adopt a dog today."

She gives a dismissive sniff at this and buries her face in Frank's fur. "But you need to feel him, Ames. He's the softest thing you've ever felt. It's like patting a cloud. Or a marshmallow."

I lean in to pat Frank, who's watching Lilly with adoring eyes, and as I get close, he growls at me. A strange little growl, like he's a teenage boy whose voice is only just breaking. What a little weirdo.

"He just doesn't like strangers," Lilly says, excusing his behaviour and conveniently forgetting that she herself was a stranger just a minute ago. "He's the sweetest dog in the world. Aren't you Franky? Yes, you are. Yes, you are," she continues, using a baby voice to lull him back into submission.

"But we must change his name," she continues, having already decided to adopt him. "Frankie is the name of my car. Hmmmm?" she says, giving the dog a long look. "I've got it! With his chocolate-brown coat and his caramel-coloured belly," she lifts him up to show me his lighter brown underside. "He's like a Snickers bar. I'm going to call him Snickers."

Franky/Snickers barks at this, and all but cements his own name change.

"Come along, Ames, let's go fill in the paperwork and get Snickers home, where he belongs."

I follow behind Lilly and Snickers with a smile, because, although the dog is a little quirky, he suits her completely. They are a match made in heaven. And now I get to have a front-row seat to watch what Oliver does when the three of us appear on his doorstep. It's going to be epic.

"Lilly, you promised you wouldn't adopt a dog today," Oliver says in a stern voice a few hours later when he arrives home to find the three of us playing in their small backyard.

Lilly picks up Snickers and the two of them look up at Oliver with their big puppy dog eyes. "Ollie, I just couldn't leave him in that place all alone and unloved. He needs me. He needs us," she says, her eyes and voice both pleading with him.

He gives her a rueful look and steps up to pat Snickers. And with that, the three of them become a family.

"Have you got anything he needs, Lil?" he asks now, patting Snickers gently, already accepting that he is theirs now. "He needs a bed, and food and a leash..." Oliver trails off, ever the practical one, making lists in his head.

"We bought this for him at the shelter," I chime in helpfully, showing Oliver the hotdog-shaped chew toy we thought was suitable to buy for him before taking him home.

"He's going to need more than toys to help him settle in here with us, guys. Come on, let's go to the pet store and get everything that he needs in one go."

Lilly gives my brother a big smile and an enormous hug, squashing Snickers in between them. I watch on with a pang of envy, knowing that while I am so happy that they've found each other, at the same time, I am completely alone.

"I'll leave you guys to it," I say, wanting to give them the space to enjoy this moment, just the three of them. "I'll call you later, Lil.

Send me pictures of this little man. I want to see and hear all about the next few days."

Lilly nods and hugs me as well. "Thanks for the best day today! Let's chat tomorrow and we can get going with the wedding plans."

"Bye, Amy," Oliver says, his voice dry. "Thanks for keeping my future wife in check today," he adds with a smile.

"I tried my best. But who am I to stand in the way of true love?" I tell him, as we both watch Lilly and Snickers nuzzling each other in blissful happiness.

"I'll see you both soon," I tell them, and I head out to walk back to my place, a few blocks over. *What am I going to do tonight?* I think, trying to ignore the pang of loneliness. I remember I have the new Colleen Hoover book downloaded and ready to go on my Kindle and think that with the right type of ice cream, my Saturday night may not be so bad after all.

CHAPTER 7

After I shower off the day spent playing with puppies, who, while being oh-so-very cute, were also all noticeably stinky, I dress for comfort in a pair of old jeans and my new favourite T-shirt, with the logo "book-clubber" printed on the front. I bought it online in honour of our upcoming book club and it's so cute that I'm considering buying one for everyone. I put my hair up in a messy bun and hop in the car, ready to drive to the local supermarket where they have the best selection of ice cream to choose from. Whilst in the shower, I had done my deliberations and arrived at two choices: one tub of double fudge chocolate and the other tub, cookie dough. The book I'd selected for my reading pleasure this evening is supposed to be a real tearjerker, so I thought it best to have many comfort food ice-cream options on hand, just in case.

Once inside the store, I grab a basket and hightail it to the freezer aisle. I know what I want and where to get it, so this should be a speedy exercise. Just as I'm almost at my destination, I see a display with the latest *Bridal* magazine and, unable to resist, pick one up for Lilly. A bride-to-be can never be too organised when it comes to wedding dress shopping. I sigh as I turn the pages with one hand, while balancing my basket in the other, enraptured by the gowns on the page in front of me, paying zero attention to my surroundings and—*Ooof.*

"Sorry!" I exclaim to the chest in front of me.

"Amy?"

Oh no, you've got to be kidding me. I know that voice. It has haunted my dreams for over two years now. I look up and up and see Lucas looking down at me, his eyes running over me, lingering on my T-shirt, a small smile on his face.

"Uh, hi?"

"Are you OK? You ran into me pretty hard just then."

"Uh, I'm fine?" Why is every sentence coming out of me like a question? Where has my brain disappeared to this evening?

"You're distracted, with...?" he looks down at the magazine in my hands and straightens up, a slight frown on his face. "Is that for you?" he asks, a hitch in his voice.

"No! It's for Lilly," I clarify.

Lucas clears his throat, and his smile comes back with a vengeance. God, save me from that smile.

"Lilly and Oliver, yes. Have they picked a date for the wedding?"

I walk toward the freezer aisle and Lucas falls into step with me, chatting to me like we're suddenly friends or something.

"Yep, in June. Only a few months from now."

"You must be excited. I know how much you love them both."

I look at Lucas and he appears to be sincere. And he has no reason not to be. From everything I'd told him about Lilly and Oliver, and everything he'd seen for himself, he knows they are a great couple and that I'm their biggest cheerleader.

"I am! I can't wait. Lilly has asked me to be her maid of honour, so I have a bit to plan for the special day."

He nods as he watches me with that special smile on his face, the one that makes me feel like I'm the only person in the world for him—Stop it, Amy, you can't be thinking like this.

"Congrats on the position. Does that mean you get to plan the bachelorette party?"

"Yes!" I gush, my excitement bubbling over at the thought. "I've so many thoughts about it. It's Lilly, so it needs to be something memorable. A night she won't forget."

We stop in front of the freezer section, otherwise known as the keeper of my dinner for tonight, and Lucas looks at the options in front of us.

"Big plans for tonight?" he asks with a laugh.

"Yes," I tell him, injecting some haughtiness into my voice. "I plan on eating a lot of ice cream and reading on the couch all night."

His eyes crinkle as he smiles back at me, having learnt from all those months ago that I've just described my perfect evening.

"Which options have you settled on?"

I point to the two I had decided on and he gives them serious deliberations. After a moment, with his head tilted to the side, he nods. "Solid choices. Double chocolate for the emotional turmoil, and cookie dough for the happily ever after?"

Damn him for reading my choices so well. Because that's exactly how I had reached this very important decision.

"Nope," I lie, not wanting him to know that he was spot on in his assessment. "Just felt like these two."

I reach into the freezer and pick up the two winners, deciding that this little chit-chat session has gone on long enough. Lucas is supposed to be ignoring me and I'm supposed to be killing him with politeness. Nowhere in my dealings with him had I factored on us bonding over ice cream on a Saturday night.

"I'd better be going," I tell him now, ignoring the way his smile drops in disappointment.

"Of course, I wouldn't want the ice cream to melt and your night to be ruined."

I nod my goodbye and walk toward the checkout, just to see him fall back into step with me. With a tart look at him, I raise an eyebrow in question.

"I'm also going in that same direction. Would you like me to walk two steps behind you?"

As I think about this, he laughs in disbelief. "Seriously, Amy? You hate me that much that you would prefer I walk behind you rather than beside you for the next minute?"

"Hate you?" I ask him, confused that he would care given the way he's been treating me this past month.

Lucas's eyes heat as he looks at me. "Well, don't you?" he challenges me now, stopping us both in the middle of the laundry detergent aisle.

"Well, don't you hate me?" I challenge him back.

Lucas looks up at the ceiling, like he's asking for patience, and then looks back at me. The expression in his eyes has me backing up a step and bumping into the shelves behind me.

He gives an incredulous laugh. "Amy, you've fought with me, ignored me and then ghosted me for almost a year and you want to know if *I* hate *you*?" He looks angry now.

I feel my face getting flushed at how he's twisting everything that had gone on before. "Ghosted you?" I demand, angry now myself. "We spent the night together, and you disappeared back to Florence without a second glance."

His face grows red at this, as he lowers his head to look me closer in the eye.

"What are you talking about? I had to leave; you know that."

"I know nothing of the sort. I leave your place, and then I get to work and Hector tells me you've gone. Moved home."

"And once he told you why, you never called. Never answered my calls," he says, his voice filled with emotion, almost like it pains him to replay this back to me.

"Why would I do that?" I challenge him, feeling the emotions from that morning returning to the surface. "He told me your girlfriend called and asked you to come home," I tell him, triumphant knowing that with this, I win any argument.

Lucas rears back like I had slapped him. "Girlfriend?"

"Yes, imagine my dismay when I found out you had a girlfriend waiting for you in Italy, especially after what we'd been doing the night before."

He shakes his head at this, clearing his thoughts, his eyes looking at me with a new kind of understanding.

"Hector told you my girlfriend called and asked me to come home?" he asks again, looking like he can't believe what he is hearing.

"Yes. So, I can't understand why you would think that I'd want to have any contact with you after that."

I watch as he processes this information, wondering why he doesn't look remorseful at all. He just keeps shaking his head in disbelief.

"What are you thinking about? Trying to find a way to excuse your cheating, dirtbag behaviour?"

"Amy, what exactly did Hector say to you that day?" he asks, instead of answering my question.

"Hector said that he received a call from Florence. Your girlfriend had called and told him you had to return home," I tell him this with complete certainty, as it's a conversation I've replayed in my head more times than I care to remember.

Lucas takes a deep breath at this, exhaling noisily. "I'm going to tell you something, and I need you to listen carefully."

I feel the beginnings of dread when he says this and brace myself for whatever is coming next.

"The morning after we were together?" he says, waiting for me to nod for him to continue. "I got a call from my *sister,* back home in Florence. She told me that my papa had collapsed and they had to rush him to the hospital. That was the phone call you heard that morning. The one that had me turning my bedroom upside down in a craze." He pauses, while I feel the blood rushing from my face. This can't be right? "They didn't know what was wrong with him. Mamma and my sister were both freaking out and wanted me to come home and talk to the doctors, and I, of course, wanted to be with them," he continues, his eyes glazed at the memory. "So, I booked a flight. I asked my sister to call Hector and tell him because I was in such a rush to pack and get to the airport. And so, she did," he finishes, looking at me with eyes filled with regret.

His sister? No. My heart stops and then starts up again, painfully beating at an uneven pace.

"Your sister? But what? How? Hector...?" I stumble, a sinking feeling in my stomach.

"I don't know the specifics. Until this moment, I didn't know Hector had thought Isabella was my girlfriend."

I stare at Lucas, trying to digest what he's telling me. His dad was sick, he had to leave in a hurry and his sister called the hospital to inform them. I'd gotten it all so wrong. *Damn you, Hector,* I curse in my mind.

"How's your dad?" I ask out loud instead.

His face brightens a bit. "He's OK, but it was a long recovery. Turns out he had a stroke, so there were many months of rehab, and I stayed on to help with his care. And to help Mamma and Isabella run the family deli."

I nod again as I take it all in. He left to look after his family. He didn't leave to go back to his girlfriend. Which means—

"You tried to call me? To tell me what had happened?"

Lucas looks away. "I tried to call you every day for a month," he says, blowing up my world with this simple sentence. "You never answered. You never replied to my emails or texts or DMs. You...ghosted me."

My eyes fill with tears at the pain I hear in his voice. The pain I caused.

"I—I'm sorry," I stammer, thrown so off-balance by this information, I don't know where to start. "I thought you were cheating on me or were cheating on your girlfriend with me. I thought—"

"The worst?" Lucas supplies.

"Yes."

"I guess it all makes sense. Now. Though I wish you'd given me a chance to explain myself then." He looks at me with reproach, which I so richly deserve.

"I'm sorry," I say again, wanting to reach out and touch him, but knowing I've lost the right to do that.

"I hear you, Amy. I think it will take me a while to adjust to this new reality. To finally getting an explanation for the way you behaved."

"I feel the same way," I stammer, hanging my head slightly in shame. How had I messed this up so royally?

"Well, I guess it's good that we bumped into each other today. We've cleared the air. We can both move on now."

Feeling this conversation was anything but good, I nod along anyway. "I'm so sorry about how it played out. I wish I could go back in time and do it all again..."

"Well, we can't do that," he says, the finality in his voice shattering my heart further. "But we can be cordial with each other at work. Make small talk in the ice cream section of the supermarket. Though I'm pretty sure that ice cream is soup now." He finishes with a little smile, nodding to the puddle in my basket. That's it. My night is officially ruined.

I laugh at his attempt to lighten the mood while feeling anything but amused inside. My emotions are in the sort of turmoil that two tubs of ice cream cannot fix.

"Cordial? That sounds good," I say, even though it really doesn't. "Let's do that."

"Great, then. I'll let you get on with your night, your hot date with the couch," he says. "I'll see you at work on Monday." And with a little half-wave, he walks away. Leaving me with a basket of liquified ice cream and a whole mountain of regret.

Later that night, after buying four tubs of ice cream—unmelted—and calling Lilly with an update on the Lucas situation, I'm on the couch, Kindle turned on but facedown, my thoughts fixed on the past. Like me, Lilly could not believe what had transpired in the supermarket. That what had been a firmly entrenched belief that Lucas was a cheating jerk is, in fact, wrong. Hearing the distress in my voice, she offered to come over for a girls' night debrief, but I could hear Snickers and Oliver "arguing" in the background (which would have been hilarious if I'd been in any other mood) and knew that I couldn't drag her away from that situation this time. So, I settle for pulling up the girls' group chat, taking comfort in their shock and unconditional support.

Madi: So, he's not a dirty cheater after all?

Sammi sends a GIF of a kitten looking shocked.

Amy: It's true, I got this one so wrong.

Lilly: It's not your fault!

Madi: Definitely not your fault.

Sammi sends a GIF of a puppy shaking his head "no."

Amy: My fault or not, I'm the jerk in this situation.

Madi: Yeah, maybe...

Lilly: So, what now?

Amy: Now, we are "cordial" with each other.

Amy: He actually used that word.

Lilly: That's good, it means he's not mad at you...

Madi: And you're over him, right? So cordial is good...?

Sammi sends an Emoji of a thinking face.

Amy: Yes, yes, over him...totally...

Lilly: You guys can now work together without worrying about any feelings getting in the way...

Amy: Yup.

Madi: Feeling any better?

I send a GIF of an angry kitten saying "nope."

Lilly sends a love heart emoji.

Madi sends a kissing face emoji.

Sammi sends a GIF of people hugging.

With a sigh, I put my phone down and try to pinpoint why I'm feeling so unsettled. My friends are right. I should feel better now that we've cleared the air. Now that I know the truth. I can get rid of all the negative feelings I have for Lucas. The only problem with that is now that the anger is gone, what am I left with? And that's what has me feeling so miserable, because what I'm left with is the reality that I had let my past experience colour the way I behaved toward Lucas, and now I have to live with the consequences of my actions.

CHAPTER 8

WITH EVERYTHING I LEARNT THE night before floating around my head, I force myself to get out of bed in the morning and start organising my house for my book club, which is making its debut later this evening. As I wait for the coffee to brew, I think back to what I'd done when Hector told me the news that Lucas had a girlfriend. I hadn't given him even a shred of the benefit of the doubt. Instead, I'd taken all my baggage from my relationship with James and allowed no room for Lucas to be innocent.

Feeling restless and needing to do something active to take my mind off my tumultuous thoughts, I pull up the as yet unused how-to running app and go for a run. With each step, I hear the words from last night repeated over and over again—Girlfriend. Papa. Stroke. Cordial. This running business is not working to clear my mind at all! I force myself to run faster, attempting to run away from my inner monologue detailing all the ways I'd gotten the situation so wrong, but instead, I'm greeted with the great clarity that I had let my insecurities ruin what could have been an amazing relationship, and there was no coming back from that.

After a sweaty one km slow run—I'm pacing myself, no five km for me today—I arrive home feeling worse than when I left. Clearly, exercise is not the answer. With my book club about to begin in less than two hours, I get to work organising the wine and snacks, hoping that Lilly will, in fact, bring extra treats, as I need an emotional chocolate-eating session. With everything sorted, I shower and get dressed back into my "book-clubber" T-shirt, which is a bit rumpled from my evening of turmoil last night, and a pair of blue jeans. Not having the energy to do anything with my face or hair, I put on some tinted moisturiser and style my hair into a high ponytail and I'm done getting ready.

"Amy, where are you?" I hear Lilly's voice as I'm leaving my bedroom, having let herself in. "I come bearing many gifts!"

As soon as I see Lilly in my kitchen putting down containers filled with cookies and muffins, I burst into tears.

"Hey!" she says, looking at me with concern. "Come here."

I walk into her open arms and cling to her for dear life. This is a much-needed hug.

"Shhh, you are going to be alright. Everything is going to be fine," Lilly murmurs into my ear as she strokes my back.

I shake my head at this, thinking to myself that everything is, in fact, *not* going to be OK.

"I messed up," I tell her, letting her go and helping myself to the biggest cookie I can see.

Lilly, bless her, gets out the wine glasses and generously fills them to the top.

"Yes, you did. But that was a long time ago. Help me understand what's happening here, today."

We sit down on my couch, cookie in one hand, wine in the other, and I try to articulate everything that I'd been feeling since finding out the truth about Lucas.

"I've been lying to everyone, including myself, when it comes to Lucas," I begin. "I never hated him—"

"Well, duh."

"Shut it!" I tell her, poking her with my foot, careful not to do it too hard, because this is Lilly and Lilly spills. "I know everyone knew about my little crush and how I enjoyed fighting with him to keep his attention on me. I guess I didn't really know the depth of that 'little crush' until the night we spent together…"

"How could you not know, Ames? Sleeping with a guy you don't have feelings for isn't your style. I thought once you committed to that, that you knew how into him you were."

When did Lilly become so wise? It's discombobulating to hear this coming from her.

"It all happened at once," I say in my defence. "I slept with him, acknowledging my feelings in the process, and then got the knockout blow he had left the *country*"—I add emphasis to this word, because come on, it's a pretty big deal—"to return to his girlfriend. From there, any feelings I had, I shut off. Or I thought I did."

"Yeah, maybe not so much," Lilly says, framing it as a question, when we both know the answer.

"Yeah, maybe not so much. And now he's back, and he's being nice to me. And I know the truth and—"

"What do you want from him now, Ames?" Lilly asks the million-dollar question.

"What I want is to go back in time and do it all again. All of it. From the night we met, I would do it all differently."

"Why not try to start fresh now? If you still have feelings for Lucas, why not tell him and go from there?"

"Because it's too late now," I say, feeling the tears threaten to overflow again. "His dad was sick, and he called me every day for a month, and I blocked him. There's no coming back from that."

Lilly doesn't have a response for this, seeming to understand the reality of the situation. What I did, no one can come back from.

"And besides, I don't even know where I stood with Lucas back then. He's never spoken of his feelings for me, so maybe we would never have worked, even if he hadn't left the country?"

"True," she says, warming to this line of thinking. "You guys fought all the time. And even though there's a fine line between love and hate, maybe you guys wouldn't have worked without the hate? You told me often enough what a jerk he was!"

"Yes, a real jerk. That's true."

"But so damn good-looking." Lilly has to ruin the momentum of anti-Lucas sentiment by pointing out the obvious.

We both stare off into the distance, picturing Lucas in his various stages of hotness. Unfortunately for me, I have a lot of content for this session.

"OK, so where to from here?" Lilly asks, bringing herself back from her musings of Lucas, her cheeks a little pinker than they were before.

"Now, we're going to be cordial." Man, I hate that word. Cordial. "While I try to move on. Again."

Lilly puts down her now empty wine glass and leans over to give me a hug.

"You'll be alright, Ames. Things will work out the way they're supposed to. Just like they did for Ollie and me."

I take in the shiny smiling face of my best friend and hope that maybe one day I'll be so lucky.

Lilly and I are through a bottle of wine by the time the rest of the book clubbers arrive. And luckily for me, tonight I am a happy, tipsy person. The wine has tapped into the joy centre of my brain, apparently.

"Hello ladies," I address the group, all seated in front of me, waiting for the book club to begin. "Thank you all for coming. And a special thanks to Lilly for the treats you all see before you." I stop as everyone gives her a big round of applause.

"Now, hopefully you've all read the book." I look at Lilly, who is looking off to the side, not making eye contact with anyone. "Or have watched the movie," I add, feeling generous. "And you have come ready to discuss all the wonderful themes and imagery in this book, and what it said about societal norms and the role of class and gender. And how that is still relevant in today's society."

I finish my speech to the blank faces of my friends.

"I thought Mr Darcy was hot," Lilly speaks up finally, having watched the movie and absorbed nothing of substance.

"But he's a real jerk to Elizabeth at the start," Sammi counters, much to my delight. A debate!

"He was indeed, and why do we think that was?" I ask, happy with my role as moderator for the evening.

"Because he thought he was better than everyone. But I think he only thought that for a moment, and then everything after that first night came about because of his crush on Lizzie." This came from Melanie, who has come with a copy of the book that is well-annotated and highlighted. I love her.

"You know who he reminded me of?" Natalie asks, joining the conversation after seeming to nap for the first fifteen minutes.

"Who?"

"Dr Mancini!" she says, causing me to jump a little and spill my wine.

As I mop myself up, I ask, "In what way is Lucas like Mr Darcy?"

"Well, at first meeting, he seems aloof and stuff. But then when you get to know him, he's a real sweetheart. And the way the two of you banter back and forth, it's pure Darcy and Lizzie. Arguments filled with longing and passion."

I stare at Natalie, mouth open, digesting this piece of information. This is how everyone at work saw us? Our arguments?

"Now that you mention it, you guys *are* like Darcy and Lizzie. All miscommunication and hurt egos. But in reality, you just want to jump each other's bones." Thanks, Sammi.

Unable to continue hearing my favourite book being denigrated in this way, I try to get the girls back on track.

"Umm, I don't think that Mr Darcy and Miss Bennett wanted to 'jump each other's bones,' as you so aptly put it, Sammi. I think they had a meeting of the minds, that Darcy hadn't encountered an intelligent woman like Lizzie before and that he didn't know what to do with the feelings he had developed for her."

"Exactly. He's Dr Mancini," Natalie says again. Who invited her, anyway?

"Well, what about Lizzie? She wasn't entirely innocent in how this played out," Melanie says, drawing my attention to her. "She let her preconceived notions about Mr Darcy colour the way she viewed him from the start. One small mistake and she wrote him off completely."

While the girls debate the legitimacy of this statement, Melanie's words reverberate in my head. *Am I Elizabeth Bennet?* I think. Did I make snap judgments about Lucas and then use all my past baggage against him?

Lilly, perhaps sensing my emotional turmoil, jumps in. "Well, I think they make a great couple. They challenge each other, they are flawed, they make mistakes—which they both own—and they have the grace to forgive each other. That, to me, is the makings of a wonderful partnership." She finishes this with a pointed look at me.

It is true that both Mr Darcy and Lizzie are flawed characters, and that is what I love most about them. And this business of forgiveness. I had never thought of it that way before.

"You're right, Lilly," Natalie chimes in, munching on a cookie and looking thoughtful. "The key to any healthy relationship is not being perfect but being willing to embrace you and your partner's imperfections."

My friends all nod and then talk about which actress version of Elizabeth Bennett they prefer, while I drown them out. Everything we've discussed tonight has hit too close to home, and my feelings are too raw to deal with both the fictional and my relationship woes.

"So, what book are we choosing for next time?" Sammi asks, suggesting that tonight had been a success, and they wanted to do it again.

I pick up a copy of one of my favourite rom-coms from the past few years and show it to them.

"*The Hating Game*, by Sally Thorne," I tell them with a big smile, excited that they will have the pleasure of reading it for the first time.

"What's it about?" Lilly asks through a yawn, the wine and the lateness of the evening catching up with her.

"It's about Lucy and Joshua, who work together, and they hate each other, but *we* all know that they love each other. And we get to watch them figure it all out in the book. It's so good."

Sammi, Natalie and Lilly all look at each other.

"So, it's a book about co-workers who pretend to hate each other, but really don't?" Sammi summarises while the rest of them smirk behind their hands.

I look at my friends as comprehension dawns on me. Have I been living my own enemies-to-lovers story? With Lucas? How have I never seen that before now?

"Oh, shut up! All of you! This book is amazing and has nothing to do with Lucas and me! Nothing at all!"

"Sure, just like *Pride and Prejudice* had nothing to do with the two of you either..." Lilly, the traitor, chimes in. Time to wrap this up.

"Right, you annoying women. It's time for you all to leave. I hope you all love this new book and come with many talking points that don't revolve around the likes of me and Dr Mancini."

My so-called friends laugh and start packing up, each taking a small goodie bag of Love, Lilly treats with them as they go.

I hug them each goodbye, giving Lilly an extra-long squeeze.

"Are you going to be OK walking home?" I ask as she sways in front of me.

"I'll drive her," Sammi says from behind me, shooting me a sly grin. "And she can catch me up on everything else I've missed."

I wave goodbye to my friends and rearrange the living room back into order. Once it's done, I pick up *The Hating Game* and take it to bed with me. I've already read it at least half a dozen times before, but tonight I'm in the mood for a story where a man and woman overcome many obstacles and work hard at finding their happily ever after.

CHAPTER 9

THE FOLLOWING WEEKEND, I TAKE up the role of dog-Aunty and look after Snickers for two days. In true Lilly style, when she went rogue and adopted a dog without consulting Oliver, she had also forgotten about the romantic weekend away to celebrate her birthday and their one-year anniversary that Oliver had already booked for the two of them. A romantic weekend that didn't include a skittish dog, who appears to jump at the sight of his own tail wagging. Enter Aunty Amy. The ever helpful—with nothing better to do on a weekend—sister and BFF, and now dog-sitter extraordinaire. So, this is how I find myself on Friday night, dog sitting, after another week of being polite to Lucas at work, and having to endure him treat me just like everyone else. I don't know why this bothers me so much, but I know now that I would rather fight with Lucas than face his apathy. Very much like Mr Darcy and Miss Elizabeth Bennett.

I take Snickers's lead from the grateful Lilly, who's racing out of the door, eager to get started on her romantic weekend away (trying not to think about that too much, given Oliver is my brother and all), and half-coax, half-pull the dog into the living room. Once there, I let him off his lead and we stare at each other. Me with contemplation, him with terror. The poor thing is shaking with anxiety. I lean down to pick him up for the cuddle he so clearly needs, and he backs away from me, only to hit the wall and jump a mile in the air. I decide to leave him to settle in peace and go to the kitchen to pour an enormous glass of wine. With Snickers the scaredy-cat dog as my house guest, this is going to be a long weekend.

With a glass full of my favourite wine, I wander back into the living room and find that he's made himself at home—in the coffee table. I creep toward him to avoid scaring him and find him lying flat on the shelf of the table, nice and comfortable in his safe little cave. Good, that has settled that situation. Now what to do with the rest of my night? I decide based on my recent book club discussions that I need to revisit my favourite story, to see if there's any correlation between the main characters and me and Lucas, so I grab my DVD versions of *Pride and Prejudice* and try to decide which Lizzie I'm in the mood for. Keira Knightley or Jennifer Ehle? As I contemplate this, I put a bag of popcorn in the microwave and place a platter of my favourite chocolates—Snickers, in honour of my house guest—on the coffee table, taking care not to disturb its inhabitant. With the popcorn ready to come out of the microwave, I go to the kitchen to fill up my biggest bowl with the buttery goods, deciding as I go that I'm in the mood for the shorter *Pride and Prejudice* version tonight. With that difficult decision made, I go to get settled on the couch—and am stopped short at the sight in front of me. Snickers, standing next to his coffee-table home, licking his lips, with the platter of chocolates now almost empty.

"No, no, no!" I yell at Snickers, causing him to duck his head and whimper. "You didn't eat the chocolates, did you?" I ask in a softer voice, not wanting to cause him more anxiety.

He gives me a sheepish look and hangs his head—is this dog for real? I grab him and attempt to smell his breath while reaching for my phone at the same time. This is bad, chocolate isn't good for dogs. I know this from that Oreo commercial. Without thinking, I dial the number of the only person who I know will be able to help me.

"Hello? Amy?" There it is, his deep voice, filled with shock.

"Lucas!" I scream into the phone. "Help me!"

"Amy? What's wrong? Are you hurt? Where are you?" comes his immediate reply.

"It's not me! Snickers ate some chocolate and now I'm freaking out!"

"Snickers?" Lucas asks, confused now.

"Lilly's dog. I'm dog-sitting and I left him for only like two seconds and he's polished off some fun-sized Snickers bars—the little cannibal—and now I'm scared I may have accidentally killed him."

"Amy, listen, try to calm down. What's he doing now? Is he vomiting? Sweating? Shaking?"

I look at where Snickers is now snuggled into the crook of my arm, licking my elbow, seeming no worse for wear. "No, he's doing none of these things. But what if he suddenly gets worse? You have to come here and check on him."

"I'm getting into my car right now, Ames. Text me your address and I'll be there as soon as I can. And on my way, I'll call a vet and find out what we need to do next. OK?"

"Yes, yes. Perfect. Thank you," I tell him, putting him on speaker phone so I can send him my address, relief pouring through my veins. Lucas has taken charge.

"I'll be there soon. Try not to worry," he says as he hangs up.

Try not to worry? I repeat to myself as I look at the dog, now fast asleep in my arms. Is that a good thing? Should I let him sleep? It's not a concussion, so I guess a little nap should be fine? I put Snickers on the couch and cover him with a throw blanket, giving him a gentle pat on his soft head. I grab both my phone and my handy-to-have-at-home stethoscope and start googling chocolate poisoning in dogs and what to look for. Just as I'm freaking out with the plethora of terrifying information about dogs and chocolate on the internet, my phone rings. Lucas.

"Hello?" My greeting is also a cry for help.

"Ames, it's me. The vet said he should be safe. Given the dog ate a Snickers bar, and that bar is milk chocolate, which is mostly nuts and nougat, the chances are low he'll have any adverse side effects."

"That's a relief!"

"You will need to figure out how much chocolate he ate in relation to how much he weighs. Do you know how much he weighs?"

Looking at where Snickers is now curled into a tiny ball, I cannot even hazard a guess.

"I have no idea," I tell Lucas now. "I'll try to get him on the bathroom scales to find out."

"Yes, do that now. And when I get there, we can calculate his risk of having any serious adverse effects."

Lucas sounds so sexy when he speaks like this. *Focus, Amy!* I tell myself. *Your best friend's dog's life is on the line.*

I hang up with Lucas, drag my scales into the living room and am presented with the next problem. How to get this skittish dog onto the scales? I grab a piece of cheese from the fridge and, after waking him up, try to bribe him to stand still while I read how much he weighs. This proves to be a pointless endeavour as Snickers just takes the cheese and gets off the scales before they can even calibrate. After many tries at this, I give up and decide to weigh myself and then weigh myself with the dog in my arms, and it's such an ordeal that when it's finally done, I'm sweaty and exhausted.

"You'd better be the world's best dog for Lilly and Oliver," I tell him in a stern voice once we're back on the couch together, with me using my stethoscope to listen to his heartbeat. It appears to be racing, but with no frame of reference for the normal heartbeat of a canine, I can't be sure whether this is a bad thing.

"Amy, can I come in?"

Lucas. At my front door. Yes!

"Come in," I tell him from my spot holding vigil at Snickers's side on the couch.

Lucas walks into the room and comes straight over to where I'm sitting. His eyes run over me, pausing on my hair, which is now out of its customary work ponytail and hanging loose over my shoulders and down my back. His hand goes to touch me, only to stop himself in time. Clearing his throat, he looks down at Snickers and asks, "How is he?"

I drag my eyes away from him, feeling breathless just from that little almost-touch and force myself to look at our patient, who has rolled onto his back, waiting patiently for me to rub his belly, tail wagging furiously. "I think he's...OK?"

Lucas crouches down in front of the couch and gives Snickers a belly rub while giving him a once-over. He checks his eyes and takes the stethoscope to listen to his heartbeat, all the while running his hand in a soothing motion over the dog, causing Snickers to look at him with unabashed love. *Lucky Snickers,* I think.

"The vet said that if the chocolate the dog has consumed has a low theobromine content, then he should be in the clear. I looked up the level in a Snickers bar, and it's very low. So, he should be fine. I also downloaded a Dog Chocolate Toxicity Calculator onto my phone, so we can double-check his risk, as it's calculated per ounces eaten relative to weight."

I stare at Lucas as he finishes his spiel, unable to digest everything he's just told me and all the effort he has gone to for Snickers the dog.

"Thank you, Lucas," is all I can think to say, as I watch him rise from in front of the couch and take his phone out to do the calculation. This is a man who has every right to despise me, based on my past behaviour, and is instead here, coming to my rescue.

"How much does this little man weigh?" he asks, in place of acknowledging my gratitude.

"My best estimate is around thirty pounds. And the chocolate I calculated to be less than one ounce of chocolate per bar when you take away the nougat, caramel, and peanuts."

"Success!" he says, as he shows me his screen, where a big "woo-hoo" is flashing. "We don't expect to see symptoms in your dog, but continue to monitor your pet closely," he reads from the screen.

At this, I feel a wave of relief. Maybe I hadn't committed poor Snickers here to an early grave after all.

"Looks like you just need to keep him hydrated and watch for any tremors or seizures, or an irregular heart rate."

Before I can think better of it, I say, "Are you able to stay and help me keep an eye on him?"

Lucas's head whips up at this request and before I change my mind, he says, "Of course I can stay."

Uncertain where to go from here, I decide to embrace the role of hostess and offer Lucas a glass of wine. And some popcorn. As I go into the kitchen to fill his wine request, I hear him wandering about my living room, picking up and putting down objects.

"A *Pride and Prejudice* night, I, see?"

"Ummm, yes. Jane Austen's a favourite of mine," I tell him from the other room.

"Mine too."

I poke my head out of the kitchen and give him my best sceptical look. "*You* like Jane Austen?"

"I grew up with a younger sister who was obsessed with Mr Darcy. So, I had no choice. I guess my question for you is, do you prefer your Mr Darcy as played by Colin Firth or Matthew Macfadyen?"

Shocked into complete silence, I stare at him from across the room, wine glass in each hand. Unable to comprehend what he has just said, I walk over to where he's standing and stop right in front of him.

"Are you asking me if I prefer the 1995 BBC production or the 2005 movie adaptation?"

"Yes."

As I continue to stand there staring at him with my hands full, Lucas absentmindedly runs his much larger hands over my hair, something he once told me he loved. Way back when, that night in bed together, he'd told me that my hair reminded him of a curtain of silk, long and shiny, and that he couldn't get enough of touching it.

I back away from this oh-so-nice caress and try to focus. What were we talking about? Oh, that's right, the movie. Placing the wine glasses on the coffee table, I pick up the DVD cases for both options and to break the tension, I tell him, "I love them both. Please don't ask me to choose."

Lucas throws his head back and laughs at this. "You sound just like Isabella. Though personally, I think her heart will always belong to Colin Firth."

I stare at him, knowing that this discussion is doing all sorts of things to my heart, and take another step back, trying to get my wayward emotions under control.

"So, which one are we watching tonight?"

And with this simple question, my heart rate takes off again. This beautiful man is here on a Friday night, rescuing my furry guest and offering to watch a screen adaptation of one of my favourite books with me.

"Umm, the movie?"

"Let's take one last listen to Hannibal Lector's heart rate and get the movie going." He kneels in front of the snoring Snickers and listens intently to his heart rate, while I watch on, close to cardiac arrest myself.

"Sounds good to me, nothing irregular. Hopefully he's out of the woods," Lucas says as he sits down on the couch, stretching his long legs out in front of him.

I take a seat on the other side of the couch, leaving distance and Snickers to act as a buffer between us.

"Are you sure you want to watch this?" I ask, giving him one last out.

Lucas turns his head and gives me a long look, one that causes me to blush and sweat at the same time.

"I'm sure, Ames. Let's get it started."

As I press play on the movie, and begin to relax, Lucas ruins all the goodwill he had just raised by throwing out, "But who owns DVDs anymore? Seriously, Amy, even my nonna in her little village in Italy has Netflix."

I throw a cushion at his head and look at the TV screen, determined to ignore him for the rest of the night and instead focus my energy on a man who deserves my attention. Matthew Macfadyen, and his adorable hand flex, have my heart for the rest of the night.

Sometime later—between Elizabeth Bennet declaring that Mr Darcy was the last man in the world to whom she could ever be prevailed on to marry, to her feeling quite the opposite—I had fallen asleep. On Lucas. Fully awake now, I'm aware that I am stretched out along the couch with my head on his chest as he sits there, also asleep. I look to my other side to see Snickers snuggled next to me, snoring softly. What an adorable scene this would be if it weren't so completely inappropriate! How had I found my way over here? And why was Lucas's solid wall of muscular chest so comfortable? I weigh up my options and decide to extricate myself from this position without waking him up. Straightening up, I nudge Snickers, trying to move his deadweight sleeping form, only for him to growl under his breath and nuzzle in further.

"Little jerk," I mutter, as I attempt to push him again. With no luck. The dog has become an unmovable object.

"Snickers!" I hiss in a quiet voice. "Move!"

Snickers lets out a feeble bark and remains in place. Seriously?

"OK, buddy. You have to wake up!" I say, louder now, trying to impart some urgency into my tone.

Just as I think I'm going to have to pick the dog up and move him, I feel Lucas shaking next to me. Laughing at me.

"Having some trouble?" he asks in a sleepy tone.

Damn it.

"We fell asleep," I inform him.

"Hmmm," he replies, his voice still raspy. "We didn't even make it to the happy ending."

My head whips to his at this and I see that he's pointing to the screen where the credits are rolling, giving me a cheeky grin at the same time. Gosh, he's so damn gorgeous. His hair is all rumpled, his eleven p.m. shadow emphasising his perfect jawline.

"Funny guy," I tell him, making sure I fill my voice with sarcasm and not the intense desire I feel for him at this moment.

Lucas rolls his head, which is leaning on the back of the couch, and stares at me. "I had a nice time with you tonight."

"Me too," I admit.

"Maybe we can do this again?"

"Meet to take care of an ungrateful dog?" I ask with a smile.

He gives me a wide smile in return. "Maybe not this exactly, but perhaps we can hang out as friends?"

Friends, huh? I think.

"Friends, huh?" I say out loud.

"We've tried to be enemies and we've tried to be—"

I cut him off before he can go there, knowing that if he brings up *that* night, we will repeat it.

"Friends, then. Let's try that," I tell him in a rush.

Lucas puts out his large hand to shake on it. I place my much smaller hand in his—ignoring the frisson of electricity that is generated when we touch—and we shake. Apparently, now we are friends. I'm in so much trouble.

CHAPTER 10

THE WEEKEND WITH SNICKERS KEEPING me company turns out to be a good one. After Lucas left us on Friday night, I put him to bed on his doggie pillow on the floor next to me, and then woke up to his body curled into mine. It wasn't an unpleasant way to wake up. And from there, we spent the rest of the weekend stuck like glue to each other. Everywhere I went, there was Snickers. Going to the kitchen for a snack? There is Snickers. Going to the bathroom? There is Snickers. He's the perfect little emotional support animal and I'm sad to hand him back when Lilly comes to collect him on Sunday night.

"How did everything go?" she asks, after Snickers greeted her as if she were a soldier returning from war. The excitement is next level.

"Oh, perfectly," I tell her, conveniently forgetting the almost-killing-Snickers incident. "We had a great time, didn't we, buddy?"

Snickers wags his tail furiously, his whole body shaking with glee.

"I'm happy to look after him any time," I tell her, as she puts his lead on, ready to walk him home.

"I appreciate you doing this for us, Ames. We had the best few days away." Lilly briefly details their weekend away at a winery in the Yarra Valley region, around a ninety-minute drive from where we live. "It was so romantic. And there was a lot of wine, so a bonus there! We really needed it with all the wedding stress going on."

"Is there anything I can do to help?" I offer, feeling like a bad maid of honour.

"Not really. The only thing I need you for is the dress shopping excursion next weekend with both the mums," she says, looking full of dread at the thought of an entire day of shopping. Lilly's mum has booked us in for a full morning session at an exclusive bridal store in Melbourne and it's been causing her anxiety ever since. "I need you to act as a buffer because I just know my mum is going to want to put me in something big and frilly."

I laugh at the mental image of Lilly in a princess dress—Lilly, who loves her sneakers and jeans—and promise that I'll be there to help guide the outing.

"Thanks, Ames. You're the best!" she says, as Snickers takes off down the driveway, pulling her with him, looking like he's the one taking her for a walk.

I watch them until I can't see them anymore and then go back into my ever-so-quiet house. Maybe it's time for me to get a dog as well?

The next weekend, after a long week at work, I get ready for a day of wedding dress shopping. I'm so excited that I'm bouncing on the balls of my feet as I finish doing my makeup. The thrill I'm experiencing at seeing Lilly try on bridal gowns is second only to the excitement I will feel when it's finally my turn. And that prospect is so far removed from reality that it's not something I can even entertain. Marriage is for non-emotionally damaged people. For people who don't drive away the one man in their lives who could have been perfect for them.

"Snap out of it, Amy!" I tell myself in the mirror. "Today is not about you and your pity party. Today is all about Lilly." I nod at my reflection and put on my most comfortable sneakers, ready for a day of intense shopping.

As it's a nice day out, I walk to Lilly and Oliver's place, grateful once again that they bought a house so close to mine. When I'm in their driveway, I can hear Snickers barking from inside and a strange thud coming from the door. What in the world?

I open the door to the house, not bothering to knock and get bowled over by all thirty pounds of dog. So that was what that sound was, Snickers throwing himself at the door, trying to get to me. As we wrestle, I hug him on the ground, trying to avoid him licking my face, and I think, *What a sweetie, trying so hard to come and say hello.*

"That dog is a menace," Oliver says from somewhere above me. "He spends half the day throwing himself at the door whenever someone walks past, and the other half asleep on every soft surface he can find. He's untrainable."

I laugh at the disgruntled look on Oliver's face and pick him up for a cuddle.

"But he's so soft and cute," I tell him, pointing Snickers's little innocent face at him.

"Don't you start too, I get that all day from Lilly," he says, giving the dog a gentle pat.

"Oh, you're a big softie," I say as I watch Snickers lick Oliver's hand and Oliver laugh in reply. "You love him."

"I don't have a choice. He and Lilly come as a pair now. And we all know how much I love Lilly."

I smile at my brother, delighted at how open he now is about his feelings for my best friend.

"Hey Amy," Lilly enters the room wearing mismatched shoes. How's that even possible? "I don't think I can come today. Snickers is sick."

Oliver raises his eyebrows at me and leaves the two of us alone. I know Lilly hates shopping, but even she can't get out of choosing her own wedding dress.

"He looks fine to me, Lil," I say, looking at the healthy dog in my arms.

"He threw up this morning," Lilly fills me in, taking Snickers from me and cradling him in her arms.

"Tell her what he threw up," Oliver shouts from the kitchen.

Lilly grimaces. "He threw up a sock," she says, stroking his back in a soothing motion. A sock?

"And tell her what else," Oliver yells again from the other room.

"Well, he threw up the first one yesterday. So, we're thinking he swallowed the pair?"

At this, I try to hold in a laugh because Lilly looks distressed, but it's just too funny. What kind of weirdo dog swallows not just one, but two socks?

"That's good. That means there won't be any more throwing up, presumably? Any other bits of clothing missing?"

"It's not funny! What if he's got something else in there?"

"Then he will throw that up too, just like the socks," Oliver says from the doorway. "We called the vet, and he said Snickers will be fine. You have to go today; our mums will be waiting."

I nod as Lilly continues to look uncertain.

"I'll watch him closely today and make sure he's doing well," Oliver offers, his eyes softening as he looks at his future wife.

"And you'll send me hourly updates? No! Half hourly?"

"Yes, Lilly. I'll send you regular updates. Now off you go, do your shopping. Your two guys will be here waiting for you when you get back."

She hands Snickers over to Oliver and gives him a kiss. I look away from the scene, feeling a pang of envy. I'm so happy for them, but sometimes their "togetherness" is just too much.

"Well, Ames. Might as well let the torture begin."

"That's the spirit," I say, linking my arm through hers and pulling her to the door. "Let's go find you the perfect dress!"

As we drive to the first bridal store where we are meeting my mum and Lilly's mum, I fill her in on the week at work with Lucas.

"So, you guys are friends now?" she asks, confused.

"We are. Apparently."

"What does that look like?"

"A friendly wave in the hallway. A smile in the break room. A chat at the nurses' desk. I found out that he also loves *The Office.* So, we've chatted about that. It's all very disconcerting. I don't know what to make of it."

"You should be glad. After everything, and I mean everything, that's transpired between the two of you, this is a great place to be," she says, looking at me closely.

"I know, but what if I don't want to be just friends?" I ask, happy to get that out in the open.

"That's not your decision to make, Ames," Lilly tells me, her voice filled with regret. "Like we discussed last weekend, with what went down after he left? That may not be something he can get over."

"I know, you're right. And a friendship is better than nothing, right?"

"Absolutely. You can never have too many friends."

I force a smile at this and change the subject.

"What are you hoping to get done today?"

"I'm hoping to find a dress in the first store we go to, the one where Mum has booked us an appointment. So that we can finish shopping early and go out for lunch?"

I laugh at this and reach over to squeeze her hand.

"That won't happen," I tell her, pointing to where the mums are waiting in front of the store, their faces beaming with excitement. "Those two are going to milk this day for all it's worth!"

"Hi girls!" my mum yells from where she's standing, a stack of bridal magazines in her hands. Oh boy, Lilly is in for an afternoon of pain.

"Hi Mum, hi Diane," Lilly says, getting out of the car and giving them both a hug.

"Amy, we're so grateful you managed to get Lilly here today. We had a bet going that she would find an excuse to not turn up," Lilly's mum Judy says with a knowing smile.

I shoot Lilly an amused glance. "Happy to be of service. I can't wait to see her in every dress in this store."

"Oh yes!" my mum squeals. "It's going to be the best day!"

The mums walk into the store, while Lilly mouths "I'm going to kill you" to me behind their backs.

"Come along, Lil. It won't be that bad."

Turns out, I was right. The first store had nothing that Lilly loved, but we had a blast forcing her to try on every dress available.

I lapped up her grumpiness, taking photos and encouraging the mums to be as obnoxious as possible.

"You know I'm going to do this to you when it's your turn, right?" Lilly threatens, her head stuck in the bodice of a dress as she attempts to wiggle out of it.

"My turn, hey?" I say, helping her out of the dress and taking in her flushed face. "I wouldn't hold my breath for that day."

Before she can respond, my mum, who has superhuman hearing, pipes up from the other side of the door.

"So, still not dating anyone special?"

I groan as Lilly gives me an apologetic look.

"Sorry for opening that can of worms, Ames," she whispers as she gets back into her normal clothes, done with this store.

"It was always going to happen. I'm surprised she lasted this long." I make a face at Lilly and open the door to the dressing room we were crowded into. *Here goes nothing.*

"No, Mum, nobody special at the moment," I say, hoping to shut this down.

She looks crestfallen. "No one at all?"

"Umm, I mean I go on dates..." I lie, as Lilly looks at me, confused. "But haven't met anyone special yet."

"You've got time, you're young, there's no rush," Judy chimes in, coming to my defence. I love her.

"That's right. And I'm focussing on my career at the moment, so I don't really have the time for a relationship."

"That's wonderful news," Judy says, while my mum looks grumpy. Boy, she's tough to impress.

"Yes, I'm applying for a new position. I'm hoping to be promoted to Chief Nursing Officer for the entire emergency department, including the trauma unit. These roles tend to go to nurses with at least a decade more experience than me, but my current boss says

I'm in with a good chance. That my works has been exemplary over the years."

"Well then, I'm so proud of you Amy," my mum says now, getting on board. "Let me know how you go; this is a huge deal for you."

"It is! You're a very accomplished young lady," Judy adds, while I feel the glow from their praise.

"Guys, I think I found it!" Lilly says, coming up from behind us, a dress in her hand.

-"It was over there in the back, behind all the big meringue dresses. What do you think? Should I try it on?"

"Of course!" the three of us yell together.

"Give me a minute, then."

We wait as Lilly is helped into her dress, each of us sipping our complimentary champagne, buzzing with anticipation.

"I'm coming out," Lilly yells, her voice an octave higher with excitement.

We all watch as she floats out of the dressing room, a vision in white. Think: Pippa Middleton's bridesmaid's dress at Princess Kate's wedding to Prince William. Scooped neckline, fitted all the way to the ground, capped sleeves and a billion buttons down the back. The fabric is satin, and it looks like heavy cream has been poured over Lilly's body. The dress is perfect for her.

"Well?" she asks when we all just stand there staring at her. "What do you think?"

My eyes fill with tears as Lilly's mum steps forward to hug her.

"You are beautiful. The dress is perfect," Judy says, tears running down her face.

Lilly looks at me. "Ames? Do you like it?"

"Like it? I freaking love it! You're the most beautiful bride I've ever seen. Even more beautiful than Priyanka Chopra when she married Nick Jonas."

Lilly's smile grows bigger at this. She knows I think Priyanka is the most perfect bride to have lived.

"So, should I get it?"

We all nod, the four of us crying and laughing and cheering.

"Absolutely. That dress was made for you," Judy tells her, gushing in a way I've never seen before. Lilly's mum isn't known for her outward display of affection or enthusiasm.

"Done. Now let's go eat!"

As Judy goes back into the dressing room to help her daughter get out of her dress, my mum looks at me.

"I can't wait to do this with you, Amy Loo. It's a day every mother dreams of."

I look down at my champagne glass and give a vague nod. *This isn't a day that's in my near future,* I think as an image of Lucas floats through my mind. Or a day that may ever happen at all.

"Let's go!" Lilly says, dress in hand, face glowing with excitement. I plaster on a smile and try to put my gloomy thoughts aside. Today is about Lilly. I can focus on my doomed love life in my own time.

CHAPTER 11

After the wedding dress shopping, or as I've coined it, the Spanish inquisition into my love life, I had to endure a full night shift at the hospital with my "friend" Lucas, who's done nothing other than keep up his end of the bargain. Just like I told Lilly, he's being nice. Stopping to chat with me at the nurses' station, eating a snack with me in the break room, walking me to my car at the end of my shift. And it's driving me crazy. Because I don't deserve for him to be acting so nice toward me, and—here's the kicker—this version of Lucas is making me want him even more.

I let myself into my house and sink onto the couch. I'm so tired. The sort of tired where actually falling asleep will prove impossible. It's one of the many downsides of working through the night. Your body wants to sleep, but all your hormones are screaming "It's daytime, do something productive!" I don't fancy lying in bed tossing and turning, because I've done enough of that over the last few weeks—thanks Lucas—and so I pick up my Kindle to find me an "unwind" book when my phone notification goes off. That pesky running app is bothering me again. It thinks just because I was silly enough to use it once, that I want a repeat performance. I pick up my phone to delete the app when something in the notifications catches my eye.

"Are you the best version of the person you want to be?" I read aloud. Hmmph. It would seem that this Artificial Intelligence has been reading my diary and knows that I am not the person I want to be.

"OK, you win," I tell my phone, dragging myself to the bedroom to change into some running gear, which is really the only good thing about this whole exercise business, the cute clothes. I pick a hot pink Lycra running top, which is extra tight and doing great things to make some cleavage out of my non-existent boobs, and a small pair of skin-tight black shorts, which make my legs look oh-so-long. If I'm going to be forced to exercise, I'm going to look hot while doing it.

Once I am dressed and back outside, I turn on the app and start following the instructions. My "virtual" trainer's name is Nancy, and she's a real bitch. No, seriously. She keeps telling me to push, go faster, and all this other nonsense. Clearly, Nancy doesn't know the tale of slow and steady wins the race.

I am about five hours—fine, minutes—into my run when someone falls into step beside me. On guard in an instant, even though it's full daylight and I'm in a well-populated area, I look over and there he is. With a halo of sunlight around his perfectly shaped head. The last person I want to see while I am running, and the very last person I want to see me running.

With my hand on my side stitch—boy, I'm so unfit—I stop running and look at him. He stops too, jogging on the spot and grinning at me like a fool.

"Whatcha doing, Amy?" he asks, being all cute and stuff. Ugh.

Tempted to put my AirPods back in and continue running away from him, I remember we are now friends. "What does it look like I'm doing, genius? I'm running."

Lucas laughs at this. "From where I was standing, that did not look like running."

The jerk.

"Shut up! I'm learning," I tell him, showing him my phone screen, where Nancy is still yelling at me to run faster.

He squints down at my phone. "Ahh, I see. A new hobby? What happened to your knitting phase?"

How does this guy know me so well? He must have been paying me a lot of attention back then.

I start to run again—fine, slow jog—to make Nancy stop yelling at me, and Lucas comes along, uninvited.

"Knitting wasn't for me," I tell him, panting a bit from the effort of talking and moving my body at the same time. "It was boring."

"And how's this new hobby working out for you?" he asks, not out of breath at all. He really is a jerk.

"It was working just fine. I was enjoying the solitude. Gathering my thoughts and all that," I tell him, giving him a pointed look that he ignores.

"Running is a great cardio workout and is a good way to centre oneself, clear the mind. We can be running buddies if you want?"

I do not want, I think as I limp to a slow walk. This Nancy chick is trying to kill me.

"Where did you come from, anyway?" I ask him, ignoring his offer. The thought of spending more time with friendly Lucas is not overly appealing.

"Turns out I live only a block away from you," he shocks me by saying, pointing toward where he came. "When I came back from

Florence, I moved in with Daniel. Do you remember him? He was the son of that cancer patient we had on and off in the oncology ward last year."

I know who Lucas is referring to. Daniel is kind of hard to forget. An ambulance had brought his mum into our emergency room earlier last year after a minor car accident and we had then diagnosed her with stage-four ovarian cancer. It had been an awful blow for both Daniel and his mum. We all watched him come into the hospital every day and sit with her. And we watched as she quickly deteriorated until she passed away only four weeks after her first emergency room visit. It was the kind of case that hit us all hard, and so we sort of adopted Daniel into our lives, in one way or another, even though he's a grown man in his mid-twenties. Daniel and I hadn't been in touch over the past few months, but it looks like he and Lucas remained close friends.

"I run on this track every other day," Lucas tells me now, bringing me back from my thoughts. "It's surprising that I haven't seen you out here before today."

I point to the phone in my hand, which has a big DAY 2 flashing on the screen, and he laughs in understanding.

"Ah, a rookie runner. Well, you need to take it easy. You don't want to go too hard too early."

"Believe me, that's not an option," I say as I come to a complete stop. All this talking and running has winded me.

"Want to take a break?" Lucas asks me now, pointing to the grassy area next to where we are standing.

I gaze longingly at the grass, which looks more like a soft blanket, and nod. Yes, I do want to take a break. We both lie back on the grass, staring up at the sky, and I sigh. This is the sort of exercise I can get on board with, five minutes of running and then a nap. I close my eyes against the bright sunshine and let my body relax, feeling a sense of peace wash over me.

"You aren't sleeping over there, are you?" Lucas says, ruining the moment.

"Shhh!"

"Did you just shush me?" he asks with an incredulous laugh.

I peel my eyes open to give him a dirty look. "Be quiet. We're having a nice moment. Your talking is ruining it."

Lucas continues to chuckle but does as I ask. In the silence, I look over at him and appreciate for the first time Lucas in all his running gear glory. If my outfit is—was—cute, his is positively sinful. Tight running shorts showing off his well-defined thighs and oh look, those are some delicious calf muscles, and a fitted dark blue top, which matches his eyes and hugs his chest and arms just right. Damn him for looking so good after running. I drop my gaze to inspect my current state and find a giant sweat patch down the front of my top, making me look like I took a shower in my clothes. Ugh, I'm gross.

"You look hot," Lucas says from beside me, where he's rolled onto his side to stare at me. I squirm inside as I watch him watching me, and though I want to continue along this flirtatious path, I'm not sure my heart can take a casual compliment. So, to ease any tension between us, I revert to my default; humour.

"Hot, like a melted ice cream cone?" I joke.

Lucas lets his eyes travel over me slowly. From the top of my now-wonky ponytail, over my sweat-filled top, down my shorts (a sweat-resistant shade of black), to the tips of my hot pink sneakers. And then he smiles.

"Sexy," he says in that deep velvet voice of his. Oh, my insides!

"Friends shouldn't lie to each other, Lucas," I tell him in a wobbly voice, trying to rein in the emotions he's evoking in me.

We are friends, Amy. Only friends, I tell myself. Though it kind of sounds like maybe Lucas doesn't want to be just friends? I roll onto my side, mimicking his pose, and look at him with a small flirtatious smile.

His lips twitches into a responding grin. "Would I lie to you, Amy?"

My smile fades a little at this, as I remember when I thought he had told me the ultimate lie.

"You know how sorry I am that I doubted you last year? I am more sorry than you will ever know about the way I handled everything," I tell him, needing to say it again. To have him understand my sincerity.

His blue eyes darken as I say this, and he lets out a big sigh. "I know you are, Amy. And I do understand now why you blocked me even though I don't fully understand why you never attempted to reach out, even if it was just to yell at me and demand an explanation. It was the complete silence that bothered me the most. Like you didn't care at all."

Grateful for his honesty, I tell him, "I've been in a similar situation before." Lucas's eyes flare at this and I rush to continue. "And so, when Hector told me what he did, it was like history was repeating itself and I went into a spiral. And that's all I am going to say about that." I cut him off before he can ask any follow-up questions. Now is not the time to talk about James.

"Fair enough. That makes more sense."

"I *am* very sorry, though. And I'm so glad your dad is better. Tell me a bit more about him and your mum and Isabella. I want to hear everything about her and her love of all things Jane Austen. She sounds amazing!"

Lucas's face lights up at this invitation to talk about his family and he paints a picture of life in Florence, running the family deli and his mamma's need to feed everyone all the time. He tells me about Isabella, who is dying to follow him here and find a Mr Darcy of her own. How she feels stifled in their little village, but how she would never leave their parents to run the family business on their own. He tells me about the Tuscan hills that surround his village, a forty-minute drive from Florence, describing them in such detail that I can see myself there, surrounded by the olive groves, with a pink-and-yellow sky above. Great, now I'm in love with Florence, too.

"It sounds amazing. I would love to go there one day," I tell him with a soft sigh.

"And I would love to take you there," he says, looking into my eyes. "As a friend, of course."

I find myself leaning just a little closer, and say, "Friends, of course."

I touch my tongue to my lips—to what, make sure they're still there?—and Lucas's eyes follow the movement. He leans forward at the same time I do and...

"Gah!"

"What the hell?"

Sprinklers. On. Everywhere.

We leap up, instantly drenched. Lucas grabs my hand and pulls me away from where we had been lying between two industrial-sized water sprinklers. Turns out our grassy knoll is a cricket pitch, and we'd happened upon its watering time. Seriously, what's with us and our bad timing?

"Bad timing, hey?" Lucas reads my mind, flicking his wet hair out of his eyes. Looking so sexy as he does so.

"Such bad timing," I parrot back, still looking at his lips and wishing they were on mine.

He leans forward slightly and then seems to catch himself, pulling back and clearing his throat.

"Hmm, yes. But maybe a kissing session in the park shouldn't be how friends behave?"

Why do I suddenly hate that word? Friends, great TV show, terrible in real life. "Yes, true. And that's what we are now."

"Friends, yes."

We both stand here, staring at each other, while I try to remember why we can only be friends now? Oh, that's right. Because I was a mean cow who ghosted him in his time of need. Good going, Amy.

After the silence has been stretched out and we no longer have any reason to be standing here together, I let out a sigh filled with regret. "Well, I'd better get home. I think the night shift is catching up to me and I'm dead on my feet."

"Want me to walk you home? Make sure you get there safe?"

Apparently, my friend Lucas is also a gentleman. Damn it.

"No, you keep running. Remember, you love running," I tease him, giving him a smile. "I think there's a bubble bath and a long nap in my near future."

Lucas's eyes perk up at the bubble bath comment. "Happy napping, Ames. It's been fun hanging out with you this morning." He puts in his own AirPods and takes off running, giving me a wonderful view of his behind. It's a good one.

With an audible sigh of my own—I'm so tired now—I turn Nancy off from where she's still encouraging me to run those last few minutes, and I walk slowly home. When I'm almost there, I get a message from Lucas. It's a GIF of Michael Scott from *The Office* running. He captions it "what you look like." It makes me laugh out loud. And then it makes me sad. The more time I spend with him, the more I'm filled with regret. Lucas, how am I ever going to survive being just friends with you?

CHAPTER 12

A WEEK FOLLOWING MY RUN-in with Lucas—get it?—I'm preparing for the next instalment of my book club. I'm determined to keep the group on track, and have printed a list of discussion questions, to avoid a repeat of the last time. I don't need another deep dive into the non-existent relationship between me and Lucas.

This past week at work, Lucas had returned to his friendly, non-flirty ways. Much to the disappointment of Jamie, who has become our biggest cheerleader. He's sure that Lucas is harbouring some hidden feelings for me and has been reading into every glance and every word spoken between us. Apparently, Lucas sends me lingering looks when I'm not paying attention, which isn't true, because I'm always paying attention when that man is around. Jamie seems to have also tuned in to the fact that my feelings for Lucas are not purely platonic and has embraced his role as matchmaker with gusto. He thinks if he requests Lucas's presence at the nurses' station every five minutes, that he will forget the terrible way I treated him and magically fall in love with me. I think Jamie has been watching too much *Bridgerton* and is seeing the potential for a rekindled romance where there is none (to be fair to Jamie, *Bridgerton* is amazing!)

Just as I have finished putting together a delicious-looking cheese platter and have laid out the wine glasses, the extent to which I can "set up" for an event, my phone beeps. A message. From Lucas! With my heart beating fast, I open it.

Lucas: GIF of Phoebe from *Friends* running.

Lucas: Want to join me for a run?

Grrr, why is he so charming? I think I was better off when he was treating me with apathy. Friend Lucas is dangerous to my state of mind.

I look through my options and send him a GIF of Michael Scott from *The Office* saying "no!"

Lucas sends a laughing emoji.

Lucas: what are you doing instead, lazy bones?

Lazy bones? Humph. It's true, but still, ouch!

Amy: I'm having the girls over for Book Club

Lucas: Book Club, hey? That sounds like a better suited hobby for you...

Amy: I know, right!?

Lucas: sitting around talking about books. Drinking wine and eating cheese?

I look around to see if he'd secretly installed security cameras in my house. How does he know me so well?

Amy: There may be cheese. And wine.

Lucas: Can I come?

Amy: Absolutely not! This is a boy-free zone!

Lucas: What are you, 13 years old? :)

Amy: No, but we do sit around talking about boys. So....

Lucas: ...

I watch the typing bubbles appear and disappear until finally he replies.

Lucas: Do you talk about me?

Hmmm. How to answer this one? Because we *did* spend the entirety of our last book club night talking about him. But tonight will be different.

Amy: You? No. We talk about fictional literary heroes. You don't fit in that category.

Lucas: So, I'm no Mr Darcy? Is that what you're saying?

If only he knew...

Amy: You are more like Mr Collins :)

Lucas: Ouch!

I smile, loving that he gets the reference.

Lucas: I'd better go before you call me something worse... like Mr Wickham.

Amy: I'm not that mean.

Lucas sends a laughing emoji.

Lucas: Enjoy your book club, Ames. Maybe we can run together another time.

Amy: Hmmm, maybe not.

Amy: Try to avoid any sprinklers while you are out there.

Lucas sends a GIF of sprinklers gone wild.

I send a GIF of a person dripping wet.

I put down my phone, a big smile on my face. How's it possible to get so much enjoyment from one small text exchange?

The girls arrive a short time later, Lilly weighed down with a basket filled with treats. That girl is the best! Once the food's out and everyone's glasses have been filled with wine, I pass out the typed-up notes for this session while everyone groans at me. These women do not appreciate a well-organised event.

"Amy, do we have to follow this? What is it? Guidelines to participating in the book club?" Sammi asks, reading from the print-out in front of her.

"It's just a way of keeping us on topic," I tell her, glaring at the group as they laugh at me. "To ensure we're talking about the book and not about specific people."

"You mean not talking about you and Dr Mancini?" Natalie says, a grin on her face.

"Exactly! It's a way to keep the fictional world where it belongs."

The girls all mutter under their breath, but let it go as I ask the first obvious question.

"Did you all read the book?"

Everyone nods with enthusiasm, except for Lilly, who's nibbling on her cookie and not saying anything.

"Lilly?" I say, my voice semi-serious. "Did you read the book?"

She groans and rolls her eyes at me. "No, Ms Harlow. I didn't do my homework," she says in a singsong voice.

We all laugh as we watch her pull a DVD out of her bag. "But I watched the movie. And I loved it!"

I take the DVD from her. I've wanted to watch it since they released it but haven't had the time. "I'll take this as your punishment," I tell her, with a smile on my face. Lilly will never change. She'll always be the person to watch the movie over reading the book, and I love that about her.

"So...? What did you all think of it?" I ask now, grabbing a cookie of my own and biting into it. Yum!

"I loved it," Melanie answers. "What's not to love? The main characters are smart and witty."

"I enjoyed their banter a lot. And it reminded me of you and you-know-who," Natalie adds.

"Is that what they were like at work?" Lilly asks Natalie, her eyes wide with fascination. "Because the main characters had mad chemistry. The way they fought..." Lilly finishes, fanning herself with a napkin in a ridiculously dramatic fashion.

"Oh yes. We used to all watch Amy and Lucas at the hospital and take bets on when they would finally get together."

My head whips to Natalie at this. They did what?

"You did what?"

The girls are all watching enthralled as Natalie details one specific argument between Lucas and me regarding changing glove suppliers, where everyone was sure we'd end up in the supply closet, ripping each other's clothes off.

"They just had sparks coming off them. It was fun to watch," she finishes up.

Huh? Sparks? I think back to the many, many fights we had during that year we worked together. The many times I had thought I was feeling disgruntled with him. Turns out that had just been a year's long lot of foreplay.

"I almost kissed Lucas last week!" I blurt out now, book club discussion questions forgotten.

"You did what?" Sammi squealed.

"Omg! You kissed?" Lilly says, her cheeks red with...excitement? Horniness?

"*Almost* kissed, Lilly. Almost," I tell her, trying to get them all to calm down.

Lilly pouts and takes a big sip of wine. To drown her sorrows at my failed kissing adventure?

"Tell us exactly what happened," Sammi demands.

I outline the whole running encounter to them, taking time to detail the almost-kiss in the grass, and when I've finished, they are crying with laughter.

"What's with the two of you and bad timing?" Sammi asks, wiping her eyes.

"I know, right? It's like someone has cursed us."

"So, what's happened since then?" Melanie wants to know.

I sigh. "Since then? We're back to being friends. He's nice to me; I'm nice to him. It's all very maddening."

"You know, I can't picture the two of you being 'nice' to each other. You've got too many emotions just bubbling under the surface," says Natalie.

And now it's just me with the emotions, I think, while I attempt to get the book club back on track.

"Enough about me! What was everyone's favourite scene from the book?"

"I loved the fake dating!" says Sammi, a dreamy look in her eyes.

"If you loved that, Sammi, then you're going to love the next book I've chosen for the book club." I pause for dramatic effect. "And this one is in honour of our resident fake dater, Lilly. Who, without knowing it, used the technique to snare the love of her life."

Lilly stands up and takes a bow, while we all cheer. Last year, she had asked my brother Oliver to be her fake date at her ex-boyfriend's wedding, and the rest, well, that is now romantic folklore history.

"What's the book?" Natalie asks.

I hold up my most recent rom-com treasure. "*The Spanish Love Deception,* by Elena Armas. It's about two people who work together, and they're enemies." I put my hand up to stop any comments. "And they pretend to be a couple for the weekend of a family wedding."

"I'm in!" Melanie says, the most romantic of the group. "So far, the two books you have recommended have been spot-on."

"And we can ask Lilly whether she can relate to the storyline, given it's very similar to her own," I say, loving the prospect of having the spotlight on someone else for a change.

Lilly's face heats a little, but she shrugs off the attention. "It worked out for me in the end. Who knows if Oliver and I would have ever ended up together if not for that time 'pretending' to love each other?"

We all smile at her, thrilled that she and Oliver have gotten their happily ever after.

"Oh, and Lil?" I say with a cheeky smile. "There's no movie for this one. You're going to have to read it this time."

Lilly frowns and nods her head. "For this, our treasured book club, I'll find the time."

We wrap things up shortly after this, with everyone heading home, hopefully eager to get started on the new book club-suggested reading. I'm so pleased with how my new hobby is going. It's so much easier than running! Thinking of running, I pick up my phone, which I'd left charging in the bedroom once the book club started, and see one new message from Lucas. It's a selfie of him, lying on the grass, on "our spot" with the following message attached: "Not the same without you, friend."

Sigh. Lucas, you are killing me.

CHAPTER 13

THE DAY AFTER MY BOOK club, I spend the morning organising. And avoiding. Avoiding my thoughts of Lucas, which are threatening to take over, so I put on the latest Taylor Swift album and get to cleaning my house from top to bottom. With the place looking as shiny as new, I sit down to eat my lunch, a sad sandwich, and check my roster for the next week, remembering that I have the Emergency Medicine conference this week. Two days of seminars, aimed at upskilling healthcare workers in emergency and trauma medicine. Madi had told me about it, as her company is sponsoring the event, and I'd asked Hector for funding to attend. I knew it would look good on my application for the Chief Nursing Officer position, as the hiring committee always look favourably on nurses who focus on continuing their education, and bonus—it's being held at a fancy hotel in the city. When I received the go-ahead from Hector, I'd booked myself a room, already planning my day-spa sessions and shopping trips in between lectures.

I was all excited to go until I found out who would be accompanying me. *That's right.* Lucas. As part of the trauma unit, the powers-that-be decided that he also needed to attend, and that is how I ended up with a two-day stay away with my new BFF. Ugh. With this in mind, all thoughts of a relaxing mini-break disappeared, replaced with the dread of spending more quality time with the guy I'm trying not to fall in love with. Lucas had already sent me a message to see if I wanted to carpool with him to the hotel, only a thirty-minute drive from here, and when my stupid brain couldn't think of an excuse fast enough to get out of it, I ended up agreeing. More time, in a small, enclosed space. A nightmare.

To distract myself from thoughts of Lucas staying in a room in the same hotel as me, maybe sharing a wall, I plan my outfits for the conference. The itinerary is detailed, so I can plan accordingly. Day one is lectures in the morning, followed by lunch and then an afternoon activity labelled "Survival Skills & Team Bonding." What on earth is that about? Needing further clarification, I call Madi, hoping she will fill in the gaps.

"Ames? Hey, what's up?"

"Madi, I have a quick question for you. What in the world is the survival skills and team bonding activity we are being subjected to on Thursday?"

There is silence on the other end. I look at my screen to make sure Madi hadn't disconnected.

"Madi? Are you there?"

I hear her sigh. "I'm here. And I can't give you any details. Just make sure you pack comfortable clothes. Hiking boots. Maybe something waterproof."

Waterproof? What the hell?

"Madeline Anne Russell. You need to tell me right now, what am I in for?"

"It'll be fine, Ames. Nothing over-the-top. I can't tell you any more than that, but know that I'm sorry..." she says, before she hangs up.

She's sorry? Sorry for what? I know it's useless to call Madi back. That girl is a vault for keeping secrets. Especially when it relates to her job. But damn, if this activity is as bad as I think it's going to be, Madi really will be sorry.

Unable to do any more about this secret activity, I go back to my packing list. Thursday night there's going to be a gala dinner, formal wear required. Hmmm, interesting. I love getting dressed up and have a vast array of sparkly evening dresses to choose from, but given this is a professional event, I need to find something more "business appropriate." I end up picking an understated but elegant black gown with spaghetti straps. It's form-fitted all the way to the ground with a long split and a low back. It's the type of dress that works with any figure and gives me the illusion of having curves where there are none. Dress sorted, the rest of the conference looks like it requires pretty standard business attire, and so my packing is complete. Now I just need to get through the next few days before I'm thrown into the deep end, where I will need to survive two full days in the company of Lucas "my friend" Mancini and some horrific-sounding team bonding activity. Sounds pretty simple to me.

Thursday morning arrives and Lucas is at my door, picking me up so we can head to the conference together. I had pointed out several times during the week that as the conference is being held only a short drive away, maybe carpooling was excessive, but Lucas insisted. He said it's the type of thing friends do together. He's really buying into this whole friendship thing.

As I buckle myself into the passenger seat of Lucas's car, I take a deep inhale and sigh. New-car smell and Lucas's cologne have combined to make a deadly combination. Deadly for my sense of equilibrium, that is. I pull out the container of snacks that Lilly dropped over to my place yesterday and offer them to Lucas, as a way of breaking the tension that only I seem to be experiencing.

"Are they Love, Lilly cookies?" he asks, his face alight with pleasure.

"Yep!" I say, popping the *p*. "Lilly baked them yesterday."

He takes two and gets to work demolishing them, groaning in a way that makes my stomach clench. Surely, he knows what he's doing to me.

We sit in silence as I scramble to think of something to say. Something other than blurting out my every feeling to him. I watch him from the corner of my eye, looking at his hands on the steering wheel, trying not to think about those same hands on my body.

"So, are you looking forward to the conference?" he asks me, startling me out of my inappropriate thoughts.

"I am," I tell him, relieved to have a safe topic of conversation. "I'm really looking forward to this morning's session on 'the role of nurses in trauma: how excellent patient outcomes depend on them.'"

"Oh, that presentation? I was actually a part of that two-year research study," he tells me, shocking me into silence. "I was one of the principal investigators for the trial in Florence and then continued the study when I moved here."

"You? You were investigating the role of nurses? Is that why you spent so much time watching me? Monitoring me?" I ask, finally finding my voice.

Lucas turns his head to give me a long, thoughtful look before shaking his head.

"You still have no idea," he says, under his breath. "That was part of it. You and your team provided a lot of insights into how to improve healthcare systems globally, just by empowering nurses to do more. And not more grunt work, but more decision-making. I cannot advocate for that enough."

I sit and stare at him, my mouth open in shock. He thinks nurses need more authority, when I had been assuming he was thinking we (OK, me) were incompetent. Is there anything else I can be wrong about? I really am Elizabeth Bennet, all assumptions and prejudice.

With a great effort, I force myself to stop looking at him, out of fear that I'll jump across this car and start mauling his face. Everything he's just said makes him even more appealing to me. How am I going to keep my hands to myself these next two days?

"So, tell me, do you know anything about the team bonding activity they're forcing us to do?" he asks, sending a charming smile my way, unaware of my inner turmoil.

"No idea, though not from lack of trying," I tell him, detailing my call with Madi.

"That sounds ominous," he says with a smirk, not overly concerned.

"Whatever it is, we'll know soon enough," I tell him, pointing to the hotel entrance up ahead.

Once we've parked the car and checked into the hotel, with Lucas insisting on carrying my bags, we find our rooms—luckily not too close to each other on the same floor, and with many walls acting as a buffer between us—and agree to meet downstairs in fifteen minutes.

I take that time to call Lilly for a debrief about the new information painting Lucas in an even better light. Unfortunately, Lilly has a life that does not consist of being my therapist on a Thursday morning, so I have to settle for leaving a long voicemail rant instead. Once I've unloaded my every thought on her poor unsuspecting voicemail, I stop to take stock of the situation. I need to rein in these feelings and do as Lucas has asked. I need to just act friendly. So, I take a deep breath and pull myself together.

"You can do this, Amy," I tell my reflection in the mirror out loud. "He's just a man, your friend." I nod to myself and, pulling my big girl panties up, I go downstairs to face the day.

CHAPTER 14

The morning sessions go by, with each one more informative than the next. My hand is cramping from taking so many notes, a fact that Lucas seems to find hilarious. So what if I brought my own colour-coded notebook? It will help me when I type up the notes from each session when I get home.

The presentation by Lucas's European research group is well attended. In fact, it's so popular that by the time the lecture starts, it's standing-room only. Lucas and I sit up the front and I listen, enthralled at the findings of this study, showing how important the role of the nurse is in emergency medicine. I'm glowing with pride when I see our team acknowledged at the end of the presentation and turn to see Lucas watching me with a small smile on his face.

"Thanks for that, Lucas," I gush, delighted to see the impact of the nurses I work with every day being acknowledged.

He nods. "I did nothing except report what I saw. And what I saw was a team that worked cohesively together. And you were a major part of that."

I stare into his eyes as he says this, about to throw caution into the wind, forget my earlier pep-talk and tell him everything I'm feeling in this moment when—

"Lucas?" I turn to see a stunning woman standing behind me. Small and slim with long red hair, green eyes and a beautiful British accent. She looks like a Disney princess and even sounds like a real-life princess.

"Victoria?" Lucas says, his voice filled with shock. "What are you doing here?"

The two of them catch up while I stand by and watch, feeling awkward but also too curious about their relationship to slink away. It turns out that they both studied together in London, explaining that fancy accent of hers, and haven't seen each other in years. And what's that? Oh yes, Victoria keeps touching his arm and looking at him with her big doe eyes. Who is this person?

With an effort that I will applaud myself for later, I decide to extricate myself politely from this conversation.

"I'm going to go grab some lunch, before it runs out," I say to no one in particular, given they seem to have forgotten I'm even standing here.

As I'm pointing my thumb toward the buffet table, Lucas seems to have found his manners and, after clearing his throat, he introduces us. "Vic, this is Amy. We work together over at Mercy Hospital. Amy, this is Vic, we're old friends."

I thought we *were friends, Lucas,* I think a little bitterly. Seems like, when Vic is around, we just "work together."

I smile through clenched teeth and say, "Nice to meet you. I'll leave you both to catch up. See you!" With a—fake—cheery smile, I turn and walk toward the buffet table. And then keep walking, right up to where Madi is manning her company booth, giving out information booklets and free pens. She takes one look at my face and tells her co-workers that she's taking a break. Grabbing my arm, she picks up two mini champagne bottles and finds us a little hidey-hole, away from prying eyes.

"What's wrong?" she says once we've both popped the champagne and taken a big sip.

I burp softly before pointing to where I came from. Madi peers around the corner and then back at me. "What am I looking at?"

"Lucas. With that perfect Disney princess. His friend from university, apparently," I say, taking another big sip from my bottle.

Madi takes the bottle from me before I can finish the whole thing in one big gulp and says, "So, Lucas is catching up with an old friend and you are taking to day drinking? You've got it bad, Ames."

With my arms crossed, I frown at her. "I've got nothing bad. I'm just a teensy bit jealous, that's all. Perfectly natural reaction, given my history with the man."

She gives me a doubtful look before pulling me in for a quick hug. "Ames, you *are* allowed to admit your feelings for him. I'm just confused, maybe because I've missed all the book clubs, but aren't the two of you friends now? And don't you still have a 'no dating a doctor' policy? After everything that happened with James?"

I sigh as I consider her question. It's true, Lucas and I are "just friends" and he is free to "catch up" with as many pretty women as he likes. My brain understands this. It's my heart that's having trouble keeping up. I explain this to Madi, who's watching me with sympathetic eyes.

"And as for the 'no dating a doctor' policy. I think that went down the drain when I slept with Lucas. No? If he hadn't left for

Italy when he did, we would have dated and I would have made it work."

Madi nods. "So, you weren't concerned about the impact on your career?"

Out of all my friends, Madi is the most career-focused and is raising a point I appear to have forgotten. The reason I held Lucas at arm's length for so long was to protect my developing career. Not that it matters any more. Lucas isn't interested in a relationship with me, so my career path is clear of any obstacles, completely safe.

"You know they aren't even talking anymore?" Madi says, pulling me back from my internal musings. "He's looking around, maybe for you?"

"I doubt that. He knows lots of people here, probably finding the next pretty 'friend' to talk to," I say, feeling all kinds of miserable.

"It seems there is no pulling you back from this pity party you're throwing for yourself," she says, taking my hand and squeezing it. "But luckily for you, there's an afternoon of team bonding to get you out of your funk."

Oh yes, team bonding. Great. "You need to tell me what I'm in for, Mads. Is it going to be bad?"

Before she can answer me, an announcement is made, calling for all conference delegates to be ready in the lobby for the afternoon activity in ten minutes. I gulp and look at Madi with terror, a look she is returning. Not very reassuring.

"See you later, Ames," she says, rushing away. "I hope," I hear her mutter to herself.

What have they got in store for us today?

Several hours later, I am no longer worried about what they have planned for us, as I'm too busy focussing on what I plan to do to

Madi when we return. When we met in the lobby at the designated time, they split us into teams and in a convoy of cars, we drove out to the bush, about an hour's drive away from the hotel conference centre. Who even knew such a dense forest existed only an hour away from Melbourne city? We were then each put into teams of four, and you guessed it, they placed me with Lucas, Victoria, and some elderly gentleman who claimed to have a bad heart before the activity began and wandered off to find the nearest pub.

The activity leader gave us each a "survival" pack, a list of instructions, and then dropped us all off at various places in the bushland. The aim of the activity, he explained, was to use what is in the pack to get out of the bush before dark. Oh, and did I mention he took all of our smartphones and watches, leaving us directionally challenged? I guess this makes up the "survival skill" element, leaving us all without technology and leaving *me* to deal with Victoria flirting with Lucas, while attempting to get out of the shrubland in one piece.

"Do you think there are any bears in these woods?" Victoria asks, aiming her big fearful eyes at Lucas.

I snort before I can help myself. "No bears in Australia, but watch out for snakes and spiders," I tell her, feeling petty.

Victoria jumps a little at this and grabs Lucas's biceps in a death grip.

Lucas gives me a look and hastens to reassure her. "Amy is just joking. You'll be fine. We'll all be fine."

"Not joking at all, but whatever," I mutter under my breath as we start walking. In my mind, I admonish myself for behaving so poorly toward Victoria. It's not her fault that she just happens to be flirting with the man I would like to be flirting with myself. As I look at the two of them together, I vow to do better. To not let my jealousy turn me into a mean girl.

"OK team," I say in a cheerful-sounding voice, trying to make amends for my earlier snark. "We have a compass, map, one water bottle, and a protein bar," I say, as I pull each item out of the bag, noting the small amount of allocated food and regretting my decision to have a liquid lunch. "This is all we have?" I ask, shaking the pack upside down to see if anything else falls out.

Lucas leans down and picks up the map and compass. "This shouldn't be too hard," he states, already figuring out how to orientate himself on the map. For my part, I take a step back, knowing that I'll be next to useless in this challenge. Me and maps do not work. That is why some smart person invented GPS.

Victoria, on the other hand, seems to have been Christopher Columbus in her past life, and is using the compass to help guide Lucas's position on the map. *Don't the two of them make an adorable little explorer team,* I think as I lag behind them, feeling more and more irrelevant by the second. I'm going to kill Madi when I get back!

"We need to go this way," Lucas says, taking the lead. He puts the useless "survival pack" on his back and starts off in one direction, Victoria hot on his heels. Not wanting to feel like a third wheel on what looks like a delightful first date for the two of them, I slow my pace and look around me. Distracted by how tall the trees are—so tall they block any view of the sky—I don't see the thick tree root in front of me and down I go.

"Argghhhh!" I yell, as I fall none-too-gracefully to the ground, scrapping my knee and twisting my ankle as I go.

"Amy!" Lucas shouts from up ahead, his voice urgent. "Are you OK?"

Before I can answer, Lucas is on the ground next to me, gently running his hand over my head and neck.

"Did you hit your head when you fell?" he asks, his eyes filled with concern.

I stare into his blue eyes and am rendered mute. What did he ask me again?

"Amy? Can you hear me?" Lucas's voice is full of something. Is that fear? And it snaps me out of my daze.

"I—I think I'm OK? Just a bit banged up," I tell him, my voice wobbly as I look down at my bloody knees poking through my torn leggings. Damn, I really liked these leggings. They do great things for my butt.

"That they do," Lucas whispers to me, alerting me to the fact that I'd said that last part out loud.

I look up at Lucas, whose face is close to mine, his eyes still worried, though he's now smiling at me, and I can't help but smile back. We stay here looking at each other until Victoria clears her throat, breaking the moment and bringing us back to reality.

"Do you think you can walk?" she asks, giving me a dirty look while Lucas helps me to my feet.

"I'm sure I can," I reassure them both, as they watch me take my first couple of steps and wince. "Or maybe not?" I add, as a jolt of pain radiates up my leg. I look down to see that my ankle is now swollen and looking purple.

Lucas takes my foot into his professional hands and checks it out, declaring it a sprained ankle.

"Do we have anything at all in the survival pack that I can use as a bandage?" I ask, feeling sorry for my poor ankle.

Lucas rummages through the bag again and swears under his breath. "There's nothing here," he says, his tone tight with anger. "There's no way they should be able to send us out here without the basic first aid supplies. This is pure negligence."

He's so worked up that I put my hand on his arm to calm him down. "It'll be fine, Lucas. I'll just limp my way out of here."

He gives me a sweeping glance, taking in my awkward one-legged stance and my face twisted in pain, and swears again. Without another word, he hands the map and compass to the almost forgotten Victoria, who's been watching this all unfold with a sour look on her face, and sweeps me up into his arms. Shocked, I grab hold of his biceps—such nice biceps—and steady myself.

"Lucas! Put me down. There's no way you can carry me out of here," I tell him.

He ignores me, focussing on Victoria instead. "Vic, are you able to lead us out of here?"

She mutters something under her breath that sounds a lot like "the sooner the better" and takes off ahead of us.

Lucas hikes me up higher into his arms, cradling me like I am precious cargo, and takes off after her.

"Stop it, I can walk. This is so unnecessary!" I protest weakly.

"Amy, stop wiggling and accept that I'm carrying you out of here." He stops walking and looks down at me, his eyes serious. "You've hurt yourself. Let me take care of you."

Rendered speechless again, I nod and rest my head on his chest. If he insists on doing this, who am I not to enjoy every minute?

Turns out minutes is all we have, as Victoria expertly leads us out of the woods and back to our meeting spot in less than five. *They really oversold this whole* survival *experience.* As we approach the activity lead, who comes rushing up to us when he sees the walking wounded, Lucas places me on the ground, keeping me close to him with his arm locked around my waist, still absorbing much of my body weight.

"You and your team need to provide the participants with a first aid kit and some sort of radio in case someone injures themselves," Lucas says, launching into an angry tirade and causing the poor activity lead to turn red and then deadly white as Lucas continues to rant. Once he's done, having extracted assurances for policy changes in the future, he picks me up again like it's the most natural thing to do, and walks me to where he'd parked his car.

"Vic, are you right to grab a lift back to the hotel? I need to get Amy here to first aid to get some ice on this ankle," he asks over his shoulder, already walking away.

Victoria gives a defeated nod he doesn't see, and turns away, while I snuggle in closer to Lucas, feeling smug and triumphant. So what if I now have an ankle the size of a baseball? It's worth it to be in Lucas's arms, even if it's just for another moment. Maybe team bonding isn't so bad, after all?

Once we're back at the hotel, it turns out Lucas is correct. I do indeed have a sprained ankle and after applying a bandage and an ice pack, coupled with some painkillers, it's already feeling better. Or maybe it's the care I'm receiving from Lucas that's making me feel better? Lucas, whose gentle hands wrapped my ankle up nice and tight. Lucas, who insisted on carrying me to my room, even though I could walk, earning us several weird looks along the way.

"You can put me down now," I say after we've made our way back to my room. He'd somehow managed to open the door while still cradling me in his arms. For my part, I'm using all of my willpower to not snuggle into his chest and close my eyes to take a nap.

"Are you sure?" he asks, his blue eyes close to mine, his gaze flitting between my eyes and my lips.

I bite my lip, watching his eyes darken as he follows the movement and nod, bumping my head on his shoulder as I do.

With a deep, reluctant-sounding sigh, he places me gently on the bed, getting a pillow to put under my foot and draping me with a blanket. I feel so well cared for that I kind of wish I'd run into an injury around Lucas at an earlier date.

"Are you going to be all right here by yourself?" he says from his spot beside my bed. I look up at him and am so tempted to ask him to stay, to lie down next to me and keep me company, but then I remember he's just helping out his friend.

"I'll be fine. Thanks for all your help," I tell him, trying to inject some lightness into my tone. "I'll just take a nap and see you later?"

Lucas gives me another long, uncertain look before walking to the minibar to take out two Snickers bars and a can of lemonade. After placing them on the bedside table in easy reach for me, he leans over and grazes his lips over my cheek.

"I'm glad you're OK," he murmurs close to my ear, his voice a little gruff.

"Me too," I say back, my own voice huskier than normal.

I watch as he leaves the room, gently closing the door behind him, and sink back onto my pillow. I think about what has transpired over the past hour and how well he'd taken care of me, and acknowledge to myself that the pain in my ankle is nowhere near the pain I am now experiencing in my heart.

CHAPTER 15

After I wake from a brief nap, I call Lilly in an attempt to get myself under control. With some time to think about things, I know I have to be sensible about what this afternoon actually means. So, he looked after me? He's a doctor, it is literally what he does every day. I give myself this stern talking to while I wait for Lilly to answer her phone.

"Amy? Hey! How's it going? Survive the team bonding?"

"Barely," I tell her, briefing her on the adventures of the last couple of hours.

"So, what? He just carried you? Everywhere?" she asks, her voice a little breathless.

"Yes," I say, trying to contain my excitement. "But that's just who he is. He's caring by nature. Nurturing by nature."

"That sounds like a rap group," she says, easily distracted. "Is it a rap group?"

"Lilly, I need you to focus," I say, wanting to snap my fingers at her. Sometimes the tangents she goes on!

"Oh yes, nurturing. So, you think that if anyone else had twisted their ankle, he would have carried them up to their room and settled them into bed. Leaving them with snacks and drinks within arm's reach?"

That had been a pretty thoughtful gesture, I think, as I nibble on the Snickers bar he left next to the bed for me. "I don't know, Lil," I whine. "I can't figure him out. So many mixed signals. Long looks and almost-kisses, followed by casual greetings and let's be friends sentiments. I don't know what to make of it."

Lilly is quiet on her end and I can almost hear the wheels turning in her head.

"So, we just need to know where he stands, one way or the other. Correct?"

"Yes."

"Then you get all dressed up tonight. I've seen that black dress you packed, and it's smokin'. You go to the gala and if he treats you like a friend when looking like that, then you will know that he has shut the door on that relationship."

Lilly is back to being Albert Einstein with her clever plans. This one may just work.

"Are you able to go to the dinner with your sore ankle?"

I look down at where my ankle has already reduced to almost its normal size and think that with some more painkillers and flat shoes, I may just be able to do it.

"I'll make it happen," I tell her with confidence. "No pain, no gain and all that sporty stuff. After tonight, I will know."

I hang up and hobble over to the bathroom. If I'm going to knock Lucas's socks off, I need to start getting ready now. There isn't a moment to waste in my mission to look hot, to tempt Lucas. A mission I don't want to fail at.

Two hours and many layers of make-up and hair spray later, I arrive at the Gala dinner. It's being held in the ballroom at the hotel where we're staying, so it was only a short walk—limp—from my room to get here. I spot Madi in the corner talking to one of the conference delegates, and I sidle up to her.

"You owe me a drink," I tell her in a serious voice once she's finished her conversation.

"What? Why?" she asks, looking confused.

I pull up the hem of my dress, revealing my slightly swollen, tightly wrapped sprained ankle.

"Oh," she gasps. "What happened there?"

"The stupid team bonding happened," I tell her as we both take a glass of champagne from the waiter walking past. "But it's not all bad," I concede, telling her about the ride I got to take in Lucas's arms.

"Well, don't look now. But your knight in shining armour has spotted you and is making a beeline for us." I turn my head to see that she's right. He is walking—no, charging—over here to get to me. "You look hot," Madi says, looking me up and down. "That dress is killer!"

Before I can say thank you, Lucas is at my side, cupping my elbow, his eyes running over me, scanning for additional injuries.

"I've got to go do some more schmoozing," Madi says, interrupting all the staring. "I'll leave you two alone."

With a feeble wave at Madi, I focus my attention back on Lucas who is looking so ridiculously gorgeous in his suit that my eyes are actually watering. I've never seen him dressed up like this. I thought Lucas in his hospital scrubs was a treat, but this Lucas here may just be the best version yet.

He appears to be just as absorbed in looking at me as I am in looking at him. His heated gaze is making a slow trip starting at my toes, just peeking out from the floor-length hemline of this dress, up along my legs, flaring at the high slit, lingering on my hips and neckline, ending with my hair, which I had deliberately left down. Long, straight and shiny. Just how he likes it.

"You look beautiful, Amy," he says, his voice gravelly.

My heart skips a beat at the intensity of his gaze and I suddenly don't know what to do with my hands.

"You do too," I blurt out, my mouth running away from my brain again.

His eyes crinkle as he gives me a big smile, stepping in closer and taking hold of my arm.

"How's your ankle?" he says, a touch of concern still in his eyes.

I pull up my hemline for the second time tonight and show him the damage.

"Not too bad, thanks Doc. I think I'll live."

Lucas's smile deepens and just as he's leaning in to whisper something to me, we get interrupted by someone on the microphone telling us to take our seats for dinner. The jerk.

"I'm on table two," Lucas says.

"I'm table five," I tell him, showing him my name card with my table number on it. Disappointment to match my own flashes across his face before he masks it.

"We'll chat later?" he asks as we move toward our separate tables.

"Absolutely."

I find my seat at table five, also known as very far away from table two—which genius put these tables in order—and am pleased to see that I'm at least sharing a table with Madi. I wave at her from where I'm seated across from her, not wanting to interrupt her work conversation and note the people sitting around me. To my left is the same gentleman who bailed on the team bonding session this afternoon—smart guy—and on the other side of me is Chris Hemsworth. Wait. What?

"Hi there, I'm Gary," the Chris Hemsworth lookalike says to me with a smile.

"Ummm," I say, still stunned at the creature sitting next to me. "I'm Amy?" There I go again, sounding like I'm not sure of my name.

"Amy? Nice to meet you. What do you do?" he asks, looking interested, and also just like Chris Hemsworth.

I shake my head to clear it. "I'm a nurse in the emergency department at Mercy Hospital. And I also work as part of the trauma unit."

Chris, I mean Gary, looks impressed by this and starts asking me questions about what my day at work looks like, and what I find the most challenging part of my job. Before too long, I've managed to get over how much of a movie star he looks like and am enjoying our conversation. I learn Gary works for the Department of Public Health and so when he's asking me these questions, he is interested in the answers.

"So, what would be the number-one thing on your wish list for your emergency department, Amy?" he asks me now, leaning his elbows on the table, all his attention trained on me.

"Money. And lots of it."

Gary throws his head back and laughs loudly at my honest answer, attracting bemused looks from the people around us. I see Madi giving me a questioning glance, and when I look over at table two, I find a pair of eyes shooting daggers at me. Lucas does not look impressed. His mouth is pulled into a grim-looking frown as his eyes bounce between me and gorgeous Gary. This is interesting. Lucas is looking at me and Gary the way I was looking at him and Victoria. The jealousy bug appears to be contagious. I can work with this.

"Gary, would you like to dance?" I ask as the band starts.

His face lights up with a big smile as he pushes back his chair and reaches for my hands. His eagerness to dance with me is doing a lot for my ego.

We face each other, a little awkwardly at first, before Gary takes the lead—literally—putting one hand on my hip, the other wrapping around my wrist. I follow along, placing my hand on his shoulder, while we shuffle back and forth, my ankle hampering any chance of attempting anything more vigorous.

While we're dancing, we keep up a constant flow of conversation, and I have to admit that if it weren't for a certain someone loitering in the back of my mind and heart, I would be thrilled to be dancing with someone as engaging as Gary. But instead, here I am in Thor's muscly arms, with only half of my attention on him. The other half is wondering what Lucas is doing. Is he watching? Is he green with jealousy?

"Can I ask why there's an angry-looking guy sending me death glares from the other side of the room?" Gary asks me. Poor innocent Gary.

"Is there?" I respond, keeping it casual, denying myself the pleasure of turning to look and see for myself.

"I'm not stepping on anyone's toes, am I?" he asks, his eyes focused behind me, looking nervous. How angry does Lucas look?

"No toes, but I'm afraid a sore ankle," I tell him now, pointing to my ankle, which is throbbing a bit. "Do you mind if we head back to the table?"

Gary, a gentleman it would seem, offers me his arm and we walk back to the table where I take a seat next to Madi. "I'm going to get a drink," he tells me. "Thanks for the dance."

Madi and I watch Gary leave with a sigh. That bum is also Chris Hemsworth-worthy.

"Miss Amy, what are you up to?" Madi asks, pulling my attention back to her.

I make my eyes widen to look innocent and grin at her. "Up to?" I ask.

"You know exactly what I'm talking about. Flirting with the gorgeous man to make the other gorgeous man jealous. And it totally worked. Lucas looked like he was ready to enter a duel, a fight, a throw down—anything to get you out of that man's arms."

My head whips to Lucas as I take in what Madi is saying, and sure enough, he's looking straight at me. His eyebrows are drawn down into a straight line and his eyes are a bit angry, a bit sad.

I tear my eyes away from him and ask Madi, "Was it too much?"

She glances over my shoulder and smirks. "I think it was just enough."

I feel a warm hand on my skin and look up into the blue eyes that have held me enthralled for so long now.

"Dance with me?" he asks, his voice low and scratchy.

I nod and take his hand. I stand up and follow him back to the dancefloor, and unlike my time with Gary, there is nothing awkward about this. Lucas puts both of his hands on my hips and pulls me to him until I'm flush against his body. I link my hands behind his neck and settle in. We both sigh at the same time. How long has it been since I've been in his arms like this?

I can't resist placing my head on his chest and we slowly sway to the music, pressed together as close as decency allows in a public space. I breathe in his scent, while one of his hands plays with my hair where it hangs halfway down my back.

"Just like silk," he mutters, his deep voice making my knees wobble. "So soft," he continues, while his other hand draws lazy circles on my bare back, causing all my nerve endings to explode with pleasure.

"Hmmm," is all I can manage to say as I attempt to move closer, the tips of my breasts pressed firmly against the hardness of his chest.

"Amy." Lucas says my name as a warning.

I lift my head to look up at him and am lost in his eyes. He's looking at me with so much longing that I lose my head. And I kiss him. Or at least I think I do. As I am going in for the kill, someone bumps into Lucas from behind, causing his nose to make contact with my lips. And then there is blood. So much blood.

"Amy!?" Lucas mutters, holding his nose, which is dripping blood. "Are you OK?"

Am I OK? I think as I assess the damage. Oh yes, I have a bloody, fat lip. Fantastic.

"We'd better get some ice for your lip. And my nose," Lucas says, taking charge while I just stand there staring at him hopelessly. Even with my lip pouring out blood, I still want to kiss him.

Madi comes over with two ice packs and a face that tells me she is dying to laugh. The biatch!

"Here you go, love birds," she says, having witnessed the whole thing and finding it all so hilarious.

"Thanks, Mads," I say, feeling all sorts of embarrassed. "Umm, maybe you should help me to my room, ensure I don't get into any more accidents?" I tell her, giving her a meaningful look. SOS, I need to get out of here!

"Let's go," she says, taking the hint and also taking my arm. "Are you going to be alright, Lucas?" she asks, before we leave.

I could not look at Lucas until now, mortified by what had just occurred. Is this what it feels like to be Lilly?

Lucas, whose nose has stopped bleeding—thank goodness for that—is looking at me closely. His face is filled with something...regret? Longing? I can't place it, but I know I need some time and space to figure out what this all means.

"I'll be fine, thanks Madi. Just make sure this one gets to her room safely," he says, his eyes sweeping over me, giving me one last lingering look.

"Will do," Madi says, with a mock salute.

"Goodnight Ames," Lucas says, gently running his hand over my hair before walking away.

"Gooth nith," I mumble back through lips that are now twice their normal size, as Madi laughs at me.

"Shuth upth," I tell her, giving her a shove as we walk back toward my room.

"You two are a disaster," she tells me while we wait for the elevator. "But despite all the hurdles and injuries, I'm still rooting for you both."

That makes one of us. As we get in and ride up to my floor, I decide I need to listen to the universe and hear what it's screaming at me. Lucas and I are not supposed to be together. Tonight was the test and somehow, despite our best efforts, I think we may have failed it.

CHAPTER 16

"So, you're telling us that Lucas head-butted her while she was reaching up to kiss him? And then he had blood streaming from his nose down his face?" Sammi asks, tears of laughter in her eyes. I sit and watch my friends laughing at Madi's recounting of my "incident" with Lucas. Yes, Madi showed up to this week's book club meet—great—and I'm left wondering why I am even friends with these people to begin with.

"Yes, and then Amy's lips ballooned up to twice the size of normal, and I had to play the role of nurse for the rest of the night," Madi tells them, her face alight with mischief.

"Are you guys done?" I ask, not amused.

"Not even close," Lilly says. "Tell us about what happened before that, all the juicy details."

I groan as Madi launches into the story of me dancing with Chris Hemsworth-Gary, telling the group how jealous Lucas was and how apparently, he marched up to me, grabbing me and whisking me onto the dance floor in a fit of passion. Who knew Madi had such a wild imagination?

"It didn't go quite like that, guys. And anyway, I'm thinking that the universe is telling me to stay far away from Lucas. First the sprinklers, then the bloody nose. It's a sign!" I finish, feeling miserable about the whole thing.

My friends, perhaps finally sensing the mood, look at me with sympathy.

"Don't be silly, Ames. You've never been one to worry about signs and superstitions," Natalie tries to reassure me. "I watched the two of you dance around each other for an entire year. You are magnetic together. Eventually, the timing will be right."

I give my friends a doubtful look as they all nod along with what Natalie's saying.

"Think about how many times I almost kissed Oliver," Lilly chimes in, reminding us of the several missed opportunities she had with my brother before they finally got their act together. The first time, it was me who interrupted their moment—my bad—and the second time they almost kissed, Lilly had been too drunk to follow through.

"I know Lil, but you and Oliver were meant to be," I say, as the rest of the girls nod along in agreement. "I just don't think that Lucas and I have the same connection. We keep missing each other," I finish, gesturing with my hands two paths never aligned.

"Well, don't rule anything out is all I am saying," says Madi. "From the looks Lucas was giving you at the Gala dinner, he's not done with you yet," she finishes, waving her hand in front of her face in a dramatic fashion. I think I like it better when Madi is too busy to attend book club.

"Enough about me and Lucas. We cannot spend another book club focused on my doomed love life," I say. I need to stop spending all my time obsessing about this man. "What did we all think about the book? *The Spanish Love Deception?*"

"I read it!" Lilly says, a big proud smile on her face. "And I loved it!"

"Of course, you did, Lil. It's practically your story," Sammi says. "The fake dating was like a page out of the story of Oliver and Lilly."

Lilly blushes and laughs. "It's not exactly the same!"

"You know, Amy, you seem to gravitate to stories that reflect your own life," Natalie says, bringing it back to me and giving me a knowing look. How is the focus back on me again?

"What do you mean?"

"This story is another workplace enemies-to-lovers tale! I mean, hello? It's you and Lucas all over again."

My friends all give me a version of a smug smile while I think about cancelling the book club for the foreseeable future. Enough of this group therapy under the guise of discussing fictional romance.

"I really don't see it," I say instead, hoping to shut this down. "And anyway, none of this matters now. Lucas and I are just friends, OK? Friends who have attempted a couple of kisses recently. All of which have gone so wrong. And now we are all going to forget about it and focus. On. Book. Club."

I look at my friends, meaning business. No more Lucas talk.

"Fine. Are we allowed to veer off the topic and talk about Lilly's bachelorette party instead?" Sammi asks with a cheeky grin on her face.

"Yes, please!" Madi chimes in.

I watch as my friends excitedly chatter about the upcoming party and am relieved not to have them talking about me and

Lucas. Because there's nothing to talk about. We are friends. And that's all there is to say about that.

I get into bed later that night, having wrapped up the book club and put it on a little hiatus. My friends had seemed disappointed that I didn't have another book lined up for next time, but I think that's a suitable punishment for them and their constant need to equate the fictional world with my real world. I told them I will pick it up again after the wedding and got them talking about that for a good half hour instead.

I lie in bed and think about the upcoming wedding and the jibes my mum has been sending my way about being single. Just yesterday, she had called to ask if I was bringing a date to the wedding. Like that's my primary concern on what will be my best friend and brother's most important day. I'm already dreading this upcoming weekend with my parents driving down to spend some time helping Oliver and Lilly with the wedding planning. We're all going out for a family dinner and I'm foreseeing the barrage of questions coming my way.

Why aren't you seeing anyone?

Is there anyone nice at work you can date?

How about trying one of those dating apps?

Lilly and Oliver will try to act as a buffer, as best as they can, but ever since they got engaged, my mum has been obsessed with me getting to the altar next. There has also been talk of freezing my eggs and tick tock, biological clock. I'm only twenty-five, Mum, calm down. As I'm getting myself worked up, my face heating with my internal anger, my phone pings. Lucas. Sending me a GIF of a puffer fish with giant lips.

Lucas: This reminded me of someone, can't place exactly who...

I look at the message and laugh out loud, bad mood all but forgotten. I'm searching for a GIF or a meme of something funny with a bloody nose when my phone rings. Lucas is FaceTiming me. *Who does that with no warning?* I quickly pat my hair down, cursing myself for washing all my make-up off before bed, and answer his call.

"Hello?"

"Amy. Hi." Lucas's deep voice fills my bedroom. "I'm checking in to see how you are. I was surprised to get your message that you didn't need a lift home from the conference. And that I didn't see you at all the next day."

I may or may not have skipped the second day of lectures in favour of hiding in my room, watching Netflix and eating chocolate. And then bullied Madi into driving me home in a desperate attempt to avoid Lucas.

"You didn't see me?" I say, eyes wide with innocence. "I was there, just busily taking notes with my head down."

Lucas smiles at me, giving me a knowing shake of his head.

"I didn't see you and believe me, I looked," he says, causing my stomach to tighten with...what? Excitement? Nerves? "You disappeared into a puff of smoke. I was looking forward to our car ride home," he finishes, giving me a little pout. An adorable little pout.

"I wanted to spend some time with Madi. She's always busy, so I jumped at the chance to ride her with her," I bluff.

"So, not avoiding me, then?"

"No, not at all. What's to avoid?" I say, then curse myself for opening that can of worms.

Lucas gives me what I can only describe as a soulful look through the phone. "Amy, we almost kissed." BAM.

"But we didn't. Again. We didn't again," I say, my thoughts muddled by the look on his face. He always looks so intense when he's talking to me.

"No, we didn't. So, what, still friends?" he asks, bringing up that F word again. Why does he look so sad when saying it? It was his stupid idea to begin with.

"Friends it is." I nod.

We both stare at each other. Lucas appears to have his phone propped up on something while he leans his head on his arm, making his bicep look enormous. How is it possible for any woman to be just friends with this specimen of a man?

"I better go to sleep," I say, reluctant to hang up the phone, but fresh out of ways to keep him on the line.

He gives me a soft smile. "Good night, Ames. Sweet dreams."

I hang up the phone, watching his face turn into my home screen and sigh. I can guarantee I will dream of Lucas and that those dreams will be very sweet indeed.

CHAPTER 17

I LOOK AT MYSELF IN the full-length mirror, dreading the evening ahead with my parents, but still wanting to look cute while doing it. I smooth down the skirt of my pink dress, happy with the way it fits my body. The halter neck gives the illusion of some cleavage where there is none, with the belted waist and flared skirt making the dress both fun and flirty. I wish I had a hot date to bring along with me to make this outfit worthwhile. At this thought, Lucas's face flits into my mind and I'm quick to dismiss it. He's my friend, not someone to bring to family dinner. In fact, this past week we've barely seen each other, with Lucas working through the night, while I have had a lucky roster filled with only day shifts. I tell myself that I'm relieved not to have spent much time with him this week, but I cannot ignore the pang of disappointment I felt every day when I waved to him in the hall as I was leaving and he was starting his shift. It feels like I've been robbed of something and each night I've waited for a funny GIF or text message from him to brighten my mood, but none have come. I guess this is what it feels like to his friend. Sporadic communication at best.

With a huge, self-pity-filled sigh, I pick up my handbag and lock up the house. Lilly and Oliver offered to pick me up on the way to the restaurant, but I had the foresight to anticipate needing a quick exit and drive myself there instead. My parents have chosen a little Italian restaurant in the nearby trendy suburb of Toorak, only a ten-minute drive away, and having already looked up the menu online, I'm at least looking forward to the food, if not the Spanish inquisition I'm sure I'm going to face.

I arrive at the restaurant and gather my thoughts. Throughout the day, I've been putting together a list of topics to bring up, to veer my mum away from any attempts at talking about my love life. So far, I have lined up politics, climate change, and the Kardashians. Surely something in there can sway her attention away from me.

"Amy, why are you just sitting there? The food is waiting for us." I jump as Lilly knocks on the window, urging me to come out and face the music.

"Coming," I grumble.

"It won't be that bad," she says, seeing my face and linking arms with me, Oliver falling into step behind us. "Ollie and I will run interference. We'll talk nonstop about the wedding; your mum will love it!"

I give her a side hug, grateful for her support, while I hear Oliver mutter to himself something about people being overly dramatic. It would seem that Mr Oliver has forgotten that not too long ago he was day drinking when he was lovesick over Lilly. At some point this evening, I may need to bring this up as another distraction tool.

"Hi, loves! We're over here!" my mum yells from the other side of the restaurant, waving her hands in the air and causing everyone to stare at us. The restaurant is small and has a homey vibe. From the reviews I've read online, this place has an authentic Italian feel, the type of restaurant one would see on the streets of Rome...or Florence.

"Subtle, Mum," Oliver says under his breath, while the three of us duck our heads and hightail it to the table.

"Hi, Mum. Hi, Dad," I say, leaning down to give them both a kiss before taking a seat at the table, only stopping when I see my parents are not alone. No. This isn't happening.

"Amy, I'd like you to meet Benji. His dad used to work with your dad before he retired. Benji just moved here from Sydney, and I thought it would be nice for him to meet some new people. Make some friends. Amy, here, why don't you sit next to him?"

I look over at Benji, the man my mother is not-so-subtly setting me up with, and stifle a groan. *Mother, what are you thinking?* Benji looks to be in his early fifties (either that, or he's lived a hard life). His ginger hair is slicked back almost solid with gel product, and he's wearing a bow tie. How hard-up for a date does my mum think I am?

"Nice to meet you, Benji," Oliver says, while he and Lilly take a seat, Lilly giving me an incredulous look. *What's going on?* I can hear her ask in her mind.

"Beats me," I say out loud, causing everyone to stare at me. "I mean, feed me," I say, trying to cover up for the voicing of my internal thoughts and making things worse.

"Yes, let's all look at the menu while Benji and Amy get to know each other," Mum says, giving me a pointed look. I look at my dad, who is grimacing and looking back at me. *It's your mum's show tonight, Ames,* is what his eyes are saying to me.

While everyone is deciding what they're going to eat, with Oliver and Lilly planning to order two dishes and share—so cute—I try to avoid conversation with the old man next to me while shooting daggers at my mum.

"So, Amy. Have you ever been to Italy?" Benji asks, referencing the Italian cuisine we've just ordered, as silence settles over the table.

"Umm, no. But I'd like to go someday. Especially to Florence," I add, without thought, causing Lilly to look at me sharply. With my cheeks on fire, I attempt to sway the conversation away from me. "How are the wedding plans coming along, you two? I know Mum and Dad are here this weekend to help with some preparations, so that should make things easier."

Lilly, bless her, takes the hint and launches into all the preparation she's been doing for the dessert portion of the wedding—the only details she's played any major part in. As she drones on about different cake options and toppings, Benji pulls my attention back to him.

"Your mother mentioned you don't have a date to the wedding," he says, once again picking the moment of silence to drop this bombshell.

I send another very heated glance my mother's way, who is looking around, oblivious to the distress of her youngest child. This is just humiliating.

"My mum is wrong about that," I answer, my brain not taking part in this exchange.

"I am?" Mum asks.

"She is?" Oliver and Lilly chime in together.

"Yes, remember I told you I've started dating someone, and it's getting serious? Very serious," I tell the table, giving Lilly a look. Come on, play along!

"Oh, that's right. The very serious guy. Of course. We know all about him," Lilly says, trying her best to keep up.

"We do?" Oliver asks, like the man that he is. Can't he read the telepathy vibe going on here?

"Yes, the guy I started seeing a few weeks ago. I told you I'm bringing him as my plus-one to the wedding," I say now, as I kick him under the table.

Oliver continues to look confused while Mum looks on with suspicion.

"How come I don't know about him?" she asks.

"Because, because..." I fumble, my brain getting me back for being left out of the initial part of this conversation.

"Because she didn't want you to get too excited until she knew if she liked him or not," Lilly comes in, saving the day.

"Did you two know about this?" Mum asks Dad and Oliver, trying to find someone to corroborate this story.

My brother looks at me, clearly not wanting to get involved in the web of lies, but when Lilly gives his arm a squeeze and I give a subtle nod to the ring on her finger, he seems to remember that he and Lilly may never have gotten to this place without me.

"Yeah, Mum. From what we know, he's a great guy," Oliver says in a tone that sounds almost believable.

"So, you've met this mystery guy?" she asks, her detective senses going haywire. This woman has been sniffing out our lies since we were old enough to tell them.

"Umm, briefly?" he says, looking to me for guidance.

"We're all catching up next week for dinner. For everyone to get to know each other better," I exclaim, trying to get this back on track, unsure how we got here in the first place.

"Next weekend? That's great! Your father and I will be back down in Melbourne for my dress fitting, so we'll join you."

The three of us look at each other with panic written on our faces. What just happened? My mother has outmanoeuvred us.

"Unless you don't want us to meet this new man of yours?"

"It's not that, Mum. It's just—" I trail off, unable to think of a viable reason I won't be able to make this happen. Other than the obvious, you know, that my "new guy" is make-believe.

"Maybe meeting the parents is too much of a big step so early in the relationship?" Benji pipes up out of nowhere. Benji the saviour, who would have thought it?

"Yes! That's it. Don't you think it's a bit much for the poor guy, an evening with all of us, all at once?"

"Oh, nonsense. He'll meet us at the wedding, anyway. Best to get it out of the way in a more casual setting, don't you think?"

I watch in horror as my dad and Benji both agree with Mum, while Lilly and Oliver look at me with alarm. What have I put into motion here?

"OK, sure. Sounds great," I force out through my teeth, my smile tight and pained. "Let's lock in next weekend."

"Wonderful!" Mum gushes, her face alight with happiness. "I'm so sorry, to have brought you here under false pretences, Benji dear. It appears our Amy has been keeping secrets."

I flush bright red, as Lilly looks at me with sympathy across the table. This night is going worse than even I had predicted.

"It's not a worry, Diane. I'm happy to be out and meeting new people. Amy, I'm glad you have a date for the wedding.

Your mum was very concerned that you were going to end up an old spinster." Benji and Mum titter loudly at this oh-so-funny joke, while I slump in my seat in embarrassment. Old spinster at twenty-five. My mum has gone truly bonkers.

After we all suffer through dinner—which was delicious—and part ways with Benji and the parents, I walk to my car, sandwiched between Lilly and Oliver.

"It would seem you've pulled a Lilly," she says to me, a smile spreading on her face.

"It's not funny, Lil. I can't believe I've done this. How did it snowball so quickly?" I moan, wanting to turn back time and start this evening again. And by start again, I mean not turn up to dinner at all.

"I feel your pain, Ames. I really do. This happened when I spoke to Sebastian. One minute we were small-talking, the next I was bringing an imaginary boyfriend to his wedding." Lilly is referring to Sebastian, her ex-boyfriend, whose wedding she ended up taking Oliver to as her fake date. At the time, it was all very confusing, but look, it worked out for them in the end.

"Try not to stress about it, Ames," Oliver says now, the voice of reason. "You can just cancel with the parents during the week. Tell them the new boyfriend is sick or something. No big deal."

I glance over at the ever-logical Oliver with gratitude. He's right. I can get out of this; it isn't actually a big deal.

"Can you believe who she wanted to set me up with though?" I ask now, still in shock at the lengths she will go to getting me to couple up.

They both start laughing, arms around each other in relationship bliss. They laugh, not realising this is all their fault. If they weren't so happy together, maybe Mum would be focussing her attention on Oliver instead of me.

"Benji seemed nice," Lilly offers. "It's just, he was a little..."

"Ancient?" I finish, as we all laugh again. "Seriously, Mum needs some glasses or something. And what was with the bow tie?"

"She's not a great matchmaker, that's for sure," Oliver adds.

"At least I've bought myself some time with this fake boyfriend."

"And no one needs to know he's fake. He just needs to come down with a mystery illness this weekend and then you guys can have an epic breakup before the wedding and you'll be fine," Lilly concludes.

I hug my brother and Lilly goodbye and get in my car to head home. And as I drive home, thinking of the web of lies I've weaved and will continue to weave over the coming days, I have a sinking feeling that things may not work out as neatly as Lilly has predicted. And that maybe I started something tonight that will not be so easy to undo.

CHAPTER 18

"YOU SAID WHAT?" JAMIE SQUEALS, not using his inside voice like I've asked him to do on *many* occasions.

I look around the break room to make sure we're still alone, not wanting to bring anyone else into the inner sanctum of my life gone mad, and whisper back, "I told my mum that I'm in a relationship to get out of being set up with her geriatric friends."

Jamie lets out a booming laugh while shaking his head at me.

"And it gets worse! I'd thought I could lie to get out of having dinner with my parents and the imaginary boyfriend, but it turns out they aren't just coming for dinner. They're coming for the entire weekend, and they're staying with me."

I let Jamie absorb this latest piece of information and reflect on the conversation I had with my mum yesterday that led me here. As I had predicted, it wasn't as easy to get out of the fake boyfriend situation as I had let myself believe. When I told her that my "boyfriend" was "sick," she cheerily told me not to worry. That she and Dad are coming down for the entire weekend, and they requested a room at my place. And given this, she is sure that the "boyfriend" (name still undisclosed) will find some energy to drop by and have a cup of coffee with them. And that was that. I'm stuck now. My mum had outplayed me yet again.

"Isn't this the situation Lilly ended up in last year?" Jamie asks me now, pulling me out of my thoughts.

"Yes, but it worked out for her because she had Oliver, madly in love with her, jumping at the chance to be her fake boyfriend," I say, feeling more and more miserable about this recent turn of events. "While *I* have nothing. No prospects whatsoever."

Jamie looks deep in thought at this right as I have a bright idea.

"Jamie, why don't *you* play the role of my boyfriend this weekend?"

"Me? Amy, as much as I love you, no one is believing for a second that someone as fabulous as me is a straight man."

I look at him objectively, taking in his manicured eyebrows and his flawless fashion sense even in the mandatory scrubs we have to wear, and am forced to agree. There is no way my parents are going to buy that he's my new serious boyfriend.

"Damn!" I all but explode. "How did I let this happen? I'm going to have to call my parents and tell them I lied, and it's going to be a whole big thing. My mum will never let it go."

Besides being a human lie detector, she is the greatest holder of a grudge. Ever. She's still holding on to the fact that I "borrowed" her favourite pair of shoes when I was seventeen years old and broke one of the heels. She still brings it up now and then, to let me know that while she may have forgiven me, she had definitely not forgotten.

"Calm down, Amy. We can work this out. Let's think about Lilly and Oliver. They got away with it because Ollie was willing to play the role of 'fake date.' So..." He stops short, looking up at the doorway and smiling.

"So, what?" I ask, feeling confused. What has he got to be smiling about?

"Good morning, Dr Mancini," Jamie says to the space behind me. How long has Lucas been in the room? How much has he heard? Usually, my sixth sense picks up whenever he is within a five km radius of me. What a time for that system to break down.

"Hello, Jamie. It's nice to see you. How was the night shift?" Lucas replies, offering his signature smile.

"Crazy, as per usual!" Jamie replies, fluttering his eyelashes at him. Despite knowing that Lucas is straight, Jamie says he can't control his flirting around the gorgeous doctor.

"Morning, Amy," Lucas says, turning his full attention to me. "Are we working together today?"

I make the mistake of looking at Lucas properly for what feels like the first time in weeks, and my breath catches. He's so damn good-looking. Today, he's wearing the navy blue scrubs that make his blue eyes pop and he has a bit of stubble that gives his pretty-boy look a "bad boy" edge. It's working for both me and Jamie, it would seem.

"Yes," I breathe out at last. "Same shift today."

"Hey, Lucas," Jamie butts in, giving me a frightening smile. What's he up to? "I hear that you and Amy here are good friends. Is that true?"

Lucas gives him a bemused look before nodding. "Yes...I believe that Amy and I are friends?"

"And friends do each other favours, isn't that right?" Jamie continues, nearly rubbing his hands together with glee. A sense of foreboding washes over me. Surely he isn't going where I think he's going?

"Sure," Lucas replies, still looking back and forth between us.

"Well, Amy here seems to have gotten herself into a bit of a pickle and she may need your help to get out of it."

Lucas's eyes zero in on mine. "Are you in trouble, Amy? What can I do to help?" he asks instantly.

I shake my head at him while giving the smiling Jamie a death stare.

"It's nothing, Lucas. Don't listen to him. Everything's fine." I rush to reassure him and shut down this conversation.

"It's not nothing," Jamie interjects, causing Lucas to look at me again. "Her mum has been hassling her to get a boyfriend and has even set her up with some terrible options. So, she needs you to be her fake boyfriend this weekend." Jamie finishes his monologue in a rush.

"JAMIE!" I yell, embarrassment causing my whole body to break out into hives. This is not happening.

Lucas appears to be taking this all in, staying silent for a full two minutes while we watch him. As he's doing this, I'm itching my arms madly and wishing for the floor to open and swallow me whole.

"Lucas—" I'm about to tell him that Jamie has been declared legally insane and not to take any notice of him, when he floors me by saying, "I'll do it," shocking me into complete silence.

And so, we both stare at each other, me itching my thigh through my scrubs, Lucas looking at me patiently and Jamie watching it all unfold, a Cheshire grin on his face.

"What do you mean, you'll do it?" I finally ask, having emerged from my shock.

"I'll do it. You need help and that's what friends are for, as Jamie pointed out," Lucas says.

Jamie nods along, looking far too pleased with himself, while I try to figure out how I managed to capture Lucas in my web of lies.

"I appreciate that, Lucas. But you don't even know what you're agreeing to," I tell him, trying to get him to see reason.

"I'm agreeing to be your fake boyfriend to get your mum to back off trying to set you up with random men," he accurately surmises.

"Well, yes. That is the top line of it all, but there's so much more to it."

"So, you'll fill me in and we'll make it work," he says, looking at his beeping pager. "Incoming trauma, Ames. We have to go. Why don't we meet tonight and talk about it some more?"

"Tonight?" I ask, tying my hair up in a ponytail. "I'm taking Snickers for a walk."

Since our weekend together, I've taken to doing this once a week, for quality Snickers and Aunty Amy time. I love it.

"I'll come along. Text me the time and place and I'll meet you there," he says as he rushes out of the room.

"I'm going to kill you," I warn the smiling Jamie as I rush out after him.

What have I gotten myself into now?

I'm dressed in my bum-affirming leggings and a long-sleeved thermal top, suitable for the cooler autumn evening temperature, ready to pick up Snickers for his walk and meet Lucas for a talk. I briefly explain the situation to Lilly at her doorstep, while trying to control the crazy dog whose sole focus is to get walking.

"You did what? What's happening?" Lilly asks while Snickers pulls on his leash.

"I'm meeting Lucas now to talk about him playing the role of my fake boyfriend this weekend," I say, holding on tight to Snickers, trying to get him to sit still for one minute. *Aunty Amy is in a crisis here!*

Lilly looks at me with confusion. "You will come over tomorrow night. Bring wine. I'll have dessert ready to go and we can sort this out."

Thank goodness for Lilly. I have time for only a quick nod of agreement before Snickers is off, taking me for a walk. We walk the one kilometre to where we're meeting Lucas, Snickers stopping every few trees to sniff and do a small wee.

"You know, this would be a lot quicker if you just did one long pee, Snickers," I grumble as he stops for the fifth time in one minute. Doesn't he know I have someone waiting for me? As we round the corner, I see Lucas standing at our meeting spot, staring at his phone and looking like a snack in his exercise gear. Sweatpants and a tight top should never look this good. The slight breeze has ruffled his dark hair and his cheeks are rosy in the cooler evening air. All in all, he looks amazing and I have to hold myself back from launching myself at him.

Snickers, upon seeing Lucas, appears to remember his saviour from the movie night and takes off at full gallop to greet his long-lost friend. When he gets to Lucas, he does what I cannot and launches himself into his arms, forcing the surprised Lucas to catch him and try to avoid many doggie kisses in the process. The whole damn scene is just too cute to be real.

"Down, Snickers!" I say, in a feeble attempt to get him to stop attacking Lucas's face. Snickers ignores me, instead snuggling into the arms of his friend, all thoughts of "walking" forgotten.

"Sorry about that, he's not very well trained," I tell Lucas while attempting to extract the dog from his arms. Said dog is having none of it, stubbornly remaining where he is. "Lilly is supposed to be taking him to puppy school, but I don't think he's a very good student."

"I think he's fine," Lucas says, nuzzling his nose into Snickers's soft fur, making me wish for a second time that I could swap places with the dog. "Aren't you, little man? You're fine!"

Snickers gives him an adoring look and licks his cheek, causing both of us to laugh out loud.

"Come on, you little brat, get down. We're here to walk!"

At that word, the dog remembers his love of walking and leaps out of Lucas's arms, forcing us to walk behind him.

"Thanks for meeting me tonight," I say, once we've settled into a slow rhythm, Snickers setting the meandering pace.

"No worries," he replies, looking like a man who is happy to spend his evening strolling behind a badly behaved dog.

"So, um, about the whole fake boyfriend thing..." I start. "You really don't have to do it. I'm sure I can figure something else out."

Lucas gives me a long look. "It's no trouble for me. Why don't you walk me through how you got here in the first place?"

I sigh. Knowing there's no way to avoid it, I begin the story of my matchmaker mum and the web of lies I had weaved.

"She set you up with an old guy?" he asks, trying and failing to smother a smile.

"Shut up! She obviously thinks that any man is better than no man."

Lucas frowns at this. "Why can't your mum just understand that you don't need a man, that you're fantastic all on your own?"

"My thoughts exactly! I think she's just so caught up in Oliver and Lilly getting married that she wants to speed up the process for me. And it's driving me nuts."

"Enter: the fake boyfriend."

"Yes," I tell him. "It seemed a good way to get her off my case. But that was when I could keep it hidden from her. Now she's outsmarted me, and I need to produce a real-life boyfriend or I'll never hear the end of it."

We both stop to watch Snickers run up to sniff another dog in the park, only to run back to us terrified when that dog wanted to sniff him back. I pick up the shaking dog and give him a soothing pat while looking at Lucas from under my eyelashes, trying to gauge where his head is at.

"Well, it would seem that you need a real-life human man to be by your side this weekend. And as it so happens, I am one," he says, causing my hopes to rise just a little. *Maybe this won't be so bad after all?*

"You mean you'll do it? You'll play the role of my boyfriend for the entire weekend?"

"Sure, it can't be that hard," he says with a chuckle. "Can it?"

"I don't think so. I'm easy," I say, causing him to laugh even more. "Oh, you know what I mean!" I add, punching him in the arm, revelling in the hardness of his biceps.

"I do think that if we're going to do this, we need some ground rules," I tell him, serious now. "We don't want to do what Oliver and Lilly did when they went on their fake-dating weekend together..."

"Which is what?" he asks, peering down at me in the dimming light, his blue eyes firmly locked on mine.

"Fall in love with each other," I say, looking anywhere but him, feeling my face heat just saying the words out loud.

Lucas is silent for a long moment, so long that I have to give in and look at him. He's now holding the lazy Snickers in his arms again, absently stroking his back as he stares at me so intensely that I cannot look away.

Finally, he clears his throat. "So, no falling in love on the weekend?" he clarifies.

I nod. Yes, that's what I want, isn't it?

"Hmmm," he says, looking at me with an expression I can't decipher. "I can agree to that."

What a relief. That's what I'm feeling at this confirmation, right?

"Great, so then we have a plan," I say. "OK, there's a dinner on Saturday night. And Mum will probably try to set up another meeting with you as well. Are you sure you're up for it?"

"I'm sure. I grew up with an Italian mamma and nonna. Your mum will be a piece of cake."

Famous last words, I think.

"Then we're locked in. A weekend of fake dating. A small amount of PDA," I slip in, noting how his eyes perk up at the mention of this. "And no falling in love."

Lucas puts out his hand to shake on it, our hands zinging with electricity as we touch.

"Absolutely no falling in love."

CHAPTER 19

THE NEXT EVENING, ARMED WITH two bottles of our favourite wine, I walk to Lilly and Oliver's place, ready for a therapy session with my BFF. After the obligatory five-minute cuddle with Snickers, I find Lilly in the kitchen surrounded by chaos.

"Lil?" I ask, approaching her with caution. She looks stressed. "Everything alright?"

"Ames! Perfect timing!" she shrieks at me, frantically measuring something out while trying to stir something else on the stove. "Here, stir this," she says, handing me a spoon and pointing me to the stove.

I step up to the melted chocolate in the pan and do as I'm told. "So, what's going on?" I ask.

"It would seem that I totally forgot that I'd agreed to bake two dozen cupcakes for the charity bake sale at Oliver's work tomorrow," she replies, looking forlorn. "I only just remembered, even though supposedly Oliver has had it written on the calendar for weeks."

With a look at the calendar, I see: "Lilly: bake sale—two dozen cupcakes" written in big red letters on the date for tomorrow, along with several reminders in the weeks leading up to it. I'm not entirely sure how Lilly missed it.

"Pfft, who looks at a calendar, anyway?" she asks, while I try to hide my smile. This is typical Lilly.

"So, we bake and talk?" I ask, doing my best to help by stirring religiously.

"And drink!" Lilly adds, pouring us both a healthy helping of wine. As we take our first sip, she lays out the next steps in the baking process and between the two of us, we divide and conquer. Once we're in a baking groove, Lilly demands that I tell her what's been going on with Lucas, and so I outline the events of the past few days, culminating in our handshake from last night.

"No falling in love, hey?" she asks, as she puts the last tray in the oven and I wipe down the bench tops.

"Of course, no falling in love. That's not the point of this, remember?"

"Oh, I know. That wasn't the point of my fake-dating weekend with Oliver either," Lilly reminds me with a pointed look.

"That's different," I tell her. "You and Ollie were already in love before the weekend even began."

"And you aren't in love?" she asks, knocking the breath out of me with her direct question.

"No, I'm not. I may have been on my way there, once upon a time. Now we're friends. Sure, I may have a teeny crush on him. He's pretty great, after all. But I've got that under control."

Lilly gives me a doubtful look as she refills our wine glasses and we settle onto the couch with a plate of cookies. Snickers jumps up and burrows into the throw pillows between us, falling instantly asleep with a sigh.

"It's true, Lil. I know things got blurry for you and Ollie over the fake-dating weekend, but Lucas and I are different. We have ground rules. He's just doing this as a favour to me."

"Lucas has been turning up as a pretty good friend recently," she concedes, biting into a cookie with a groan.

"I know, right? I wish I'd put him in the friend zone to begin with. It would have saved me so much trouble."

Lilly nods and thinks about this. "Remember the state you were in when you met him?" she says, reminiscing about that fateful night over two years ago.

"Oh, I remember. I'd been so shocked that someone who looks like a Calvin Klein model would want to talk to me. Until I heard he was a doctor, starting at Mercy Hospital in the same department as me." I grimace as I think about it.

"You were so determined to hate him. To keep him at arm's length at all costs."

"And can you blame me? After what happened with James?"

"Not one bit," Lilly says, ever the loyal friend. "I guess I just wish it hadn't gone that way from the start."

"You and me both, Lil. It would have saved me a lot of heartache if I'd just been able to either date him or befriend him. I did neither and look where we are."

"Where you are is gearing up for a weekend of pretending to be in a relationship. Make sure you guard your heart, Ames. That sort of situation can get confusing really quickly. Take it from someone who knows."

I look at Lilly and nod. Guarding my heart will be my number-one priority this weekend.

My parents arrive at my place on Friday night in a whirlwind of noise and chatter. They make fast work of settling in and it's not long before I see Mum cleaning my already clean kitchen. This is going to be a long weekend.

"So, when are we meeting this boyfriend of yours? What's his name again?" she asks, while wiping down the front of my fridge.

I feel myself flush at this, knowing that the lies will begin in full force from this moment on. "His name is Lucas, and he's working tonight. You'll meet him at dinner tomorrow, as promised," I say, going to the cupboard to get some wine glasses out. I'm going to need alcohol and lots of it to survive the next few days.

"He's feeling better, then? To be at work tonight?" she asks, giving me a shrewd look. Damn it, I need to make sure I keep my lies in order.

"Yes, Mum, turns out it was only a twenty-four-hour bug. He's much better now."

"That's great news. And he works with you? He's a doctor?" Mum continues with the third degree, as I look at Dad with pleading eyes. Help me out here.

"Diane, why don't you take a breath and stop badgering the girl with so many questions? We'll meet this Lucas fellow soon enough," he says, coming to my rescue.

Mum sighs and puts the cloth down, accepting a wine from me and sitting on the couch next to Dad. "I'm just so excited to meet him. Our little Amy with a boyfriend, and he's a doctor. Isn't that perfect?"

I watch Mum's face light up and groan silently. It's going to devastate her when I fake break up with my fake boyfriend.

"Why don't we talk about the wedding? You have a dress fitting tomorrow. What else have you got planned for the weekend?" I ask, distracting them both with talk of the upcoming wedding. It's the only thing Mum is excited about other than meeting Lucas.

We spend the next hour sipping wine and talking about the wedding. I dodge over a thousand questions about Lucas and then call it a night. I'm exhausted, and the weekend has only just begun.

The next day, Lilly and I accompany Mum to her dress fitting. Evidently, the role of mother of the groom requires her to have not one but two custom dresses made for the day.

"This one is for the ceremony," Mum says, twirling in front of us wearing an elegant dress in a pale shade of blue. "And the other one is for the party!"

Lilly and I look at each other with a smile. It would appear that my mum is going to be fancier than both the bride and the maid of honour put together.

"So, tell me Lilly," Mum says as she sips on the champagne provided to us by the lovely dressmaker lady. "Have you met Lucas? And what do you think of him?"

Lilly looks at me like a deer in headlights. We hadn't thought about this part of the story—the alibi witnesses—in our devious scheme.

"Um, yes, I've met him several times," she stammers, her face going bright red, as it often does when she's lying. A fact my mum is unfamiliar with, thankfully. "He's great!"

I look at Lilly and give her a thumbs-up behind Mum's back. So far, so good.

"But is he good enough for our Amy?" Mum pries.

"Mum," I whine, drawing out the word and trying to shut this conversation down. "A man doesn't need to be 'good enough' for me. We need to be good enough for each other."

"Yes, yes," she replies, waving her hand and ignoring me completely. "But I want to know more about him. Lilly, what sort of man is he?"

I watch as Lilly's eyes dart around the room, frantically looking for answers.

"Ah, he's tall," she starts, while my mum frowns at her. "And he challenges her. He doesn't back down when she wants to be right all the time." *Well, that much we know is true,* I think. *Well done, Lilly.*

"He's kind. And nurturing. He has the same sense of humour as Amy. He makes her laugh. From the limited time I've spent with the two of them, I know she lights up when they are together."

Lilly's little speech is enough to make my emotional mum tear up while I look at her, speechless. Does she really feel this way? Is that how she sees Lucas? And the two of us together?

"Thank you, Lilly," Mum gushes. "That's more information than I have extracted from Amy over there. Now I really can't wait to meet him!"

I look at Lilly who shrugs and mouths the word "sorry" at me, and I steel myself for the night ahead. Thanks to my best friend here, the expectations for my fake relationship with Lucas are now sky high.

Right on the dot of seven o'clock, the doorbell rings and so begins the evening from hell. For me. I answer the door to see Lucas looking breathtaking in beige chinos and a long-sleeved, dark blue

Henley top, which moulds to his chest perfectly. He's holding two bouquets of flowers.

"Darling," he says, stepping inside and kissing me fully on the lips, lingering for a moment, before straightening. "You look beautiful!"

I step back, feeling breathless and tingly from the brief moment of having his lips on mine, allowing Lucas into the house, as he takes the time to give me a sweeping glance. His eyes linger on my short skirt and fitted top, smiling at me in appreciation.

"You must be Lucas," Mum says, sweeping in behind me and giving him a hug. "We're so happy to meet you."

"I'm pleased to meet you too, Mrs Harlow," Lucas responds, giving her his thousand-watt smile and making her blush. It never fails. That smile is a lady killer. "These are for you," he says as he hands her the second bunch of flowers. Mum takes them from him, giving him a dazed look in return.

"You can call me Diane, or Di for short," she says, linking her arm through his and pulling him further into the living room. "Come in and meet Amy's dad. Tom? This is Lucas, Amy's boyfriend."

I cringe at the level of excitement in her voice while watching the two men size each other up.

"It's great to meet you, Sir," Lucas says respectfully. "Amy speaks so highly of you; I feel like I already know you both."

My dad smiles, already charmed, and offers Lucas a drink while Mum and I put the flowers into vases.

"You didn't tell me that Lucas looks like that," Mum hisses at me, loud enough to cause Lucas and Dad to laugh in the next room.

"Mum! Keep it down," I whisper back, dying from secondhand embarrassment.

"Amy, dear. That man is beautiful," Mum says, with a dreamy look on her face.

"I'm well aware," I grumble, as a pair of muscular arms encircle me from behind and pull me back against a very nice, solid chest.

"Are you talking about me, sweetheart?" Lucas asks, kissing me just below my ear. More tingles everywhere.

I try to extricate myself from this embrace without looking too obvious, however Lucas is having none of it. Instead, he turns me around to face him and kisses me on the tip of my nose.

"No need to be embarrassed, honey," he says, loud enough for my mum to hear. Not that she's trying to give us privacy or anything—her eyes and ears are glued to the scene in front of her. "You know I think you're beautiful, too. The most beautiful woman I've ever met," he finishes with so much sincerity that I melt a little, forgetting in the moment that this isn't real.

"Well, aren't you two sweet together," Mum gushes. "I'm just going to go finished getting dressed and give the two of you some time to say a proper hello." She walks out of the kitchen, leaving me in Lucas's arms, a place I'm feeling all too comfortable in.

I pull myself together and take a couple of steps back, trying to get some breathing space from the magnetic energy that is Lucas.

"That was a good start," I tell him, gathering my thoughts. "But you don't have to lay it on so thick. Both me and my mum know I'm not the most beautiful woman in the world."

He throws a heated glance my way, his eyes lingering on my lips and hair, and says nothing, leaving me to stare at him awkwardly.

"And maybe we can limit the PDA? I wouldn't want to make my parents uncomfortable," I finish, trying to fill in the silence.

"No can do," Lucas responds, shocking me. "This weekend, you're my girlfriend. And there's no world in which we are a couple and you look like that"—he motions to my outfit—"and I can keep my hands to myself."

My body heats up again at this declaration, causing me to sweat and need to fan my face. "Umm," I say in response. "OK?"

"Good, glad we have that settled." He takes my hand in his and walks the two of us back to join my parents in the living room. "Let's get this dinner party started."

We meet Lilly and Oliver at a nearby Vietnamese restaurant, with Lucas holding my hand the entire car ride there, absentmindedly stroking his thumb over mine. After we sit down, Lucas surprises all of us by pulling my chair closer to his, putting his arm around my shoulder, and nuzzling the side of my neck.

"You smell good," he whispers, his breath tickling my ear and causing my heart to race.

"You need to cool it," I whisper back, trying to inch away from him, to no avail. He's determined to keep me firmly by his side.

"So, what are we ordering?" Mum asks the group, flashing Lucas a big, beaming smile of approval.

As we all look at the menu, I catch Lilly looking at me and Lucas with a slight frown. I try to speak to her with my eyes and let her know it's all under control, but even I am doubting whether this is true.

"Have you ever had pho, Di?" Lucas asks my mum now.

"I don't think so," she answers. "Is it any good?"

"Amy loves it," he says, shocking me because it's true. I love pho. "She gets it at least once a week from a little takeaway restaurant near the hospital."

Lilly and Mum are staring at Lucas like he has solved world hunger, rather than just knowing where I like to lunch. Come on, people, rein it in.

"I guess that's what I'll order, then. How about you, Tom?"

My dad looks a little uncertain, not adventurous with his food choices, and then nods.

"Looks like it's pho all round," Lucas says, ordering for the table.

Once this is settled, Mum gets stuck into the business of making me as uncomfortable as possible. She's very skilled in this area.

"How long have the two of you known each other?" she asks, spearing us both with a look.

"Ummm," I say, unprepared for even this, the simplest question. I haven't done enough preparation for this weekend.

"Amy and I met over two years ago," Lucas answers smoothly. "We've worked together over that amount of time, though I had to return home for an extended period in the middle there."

"And where is home?" Dad pipes up.

"I'm from Florence originally. That is where my family is." He fills them in on his upbringing in Italy and his studies in London. "But now I consider Melbourne home," he finishes, looking at me, his eyes travelling over my face and making me blush.

"What is it about Melbourne that has you so hooked?" Mum asks.

Lucas turns his body fully toward mine and looks into my eyes. I hold my breath and am mesmerised by the emotion I see there.

"I love everything about this city," he finally answers, clearing his throat and shifting back to face my parents. "What's not to love? The food, the culture, the sports, the people." He says this last part with another side look to me. "I can see myself living here forever."

This answer satisfies my parents, who are looking at each other with happy smiles. When I'm able to look at Lilly again, she motions her head toward the bathroom.

"Ames, feel like washing up before the food arrives?" she asks, standing up and forcing me to follow.

I feel four sets of eyes burning into my back as I join Lilly in the restroom, where she locks the door and turns to face me.

"I thought you guys put some boundaries in place?" she says.

"We did!" I answer. "At least, I thought we did."

"That man out there is acting like you hung the moon and the stars. Is he just pretending?"

"Of course he is! He's doing what I asked him to do," I tell her, convincing myself at the same time.

"Are you sure? Because after that little display, I'm pretty convinced he's in love with you."

My whole body jerks at this, startling me and making me question what I'm feeling. Do I want Lucas to be in love with me?

"Do you want Lucas to be in love with you?" Lilly asks now, her voice soft.

"No? I don't think so?" I reply. "And it doesn't matter, anyway. We're just pretending. Come Monday, everything will be back to normal. Just friends again."

Lilly continues to look at me with a worried expression on her face, but like a good friend, she tries to buy in to my delusions and lets it go.

"Your mum is going to be crushed when you guys break up," she whispers to me as we walk back to the table where the food has arrived.

I sigh and nod my head. "Don't I know it."

The rest of the evening passes in a blur of good food and even better conversation. Lucas turns out to be the perfect dinner guest, filled with interesting stories about his time in Italy and the travelling he's done around Europe. He asks questions of everyone at the table, remembering so much information about the people seated there. It's like he had a cheat sheet written up beforehand. A guide to all the things he needs to know about the people Amy loves the most. By the end of the meal, he has everyone eating out of the palm of his hand. And he does all of this while touching me in some way the entire night. He keeps up a constant barrage of stroking my face or running his hand down the back of my hair, even raining delightful little kisses down on my shoulder or cheek. It's like he can't keep his hands or his lips off my body. And I don't hate it. In fact, by the end of the evening, I've started to crave it. Every time he's touched me, I've melted into it. Moving closer to him, snuggling into the warmth of his body. If this is how he wants to play at being my boyfriend, who am I to argue?

"Well Lucas, it's been wonderful spending time with you today," Mum tells him as we arrive at the front door of my house. "Please don't feel you have to leave because Tom and I are here. We are modern parents, after all. We know that you and Amy have been...how should I put this? Intimate?"

And just like that, I die. On the spot.

Lucas has the audacity to laugh at this, not even having the grace to blush. "I appreciate that, Di. But I have an early start at the hospital tomorrow morning, so I should get home."

She smiles at him and pats his cheek. "But I insist you come for afternoon tea tomorrow if you finish work on time. I simply must spend some more time with you before we leave."

Lucas looks at me, his eyebrow raised in question, and I nod in resignation. There's no way we are getting out of at least one more catch-up this weekend.

"I would love to, Di. Is there anything I can bring with me? Perhaps I can stop at Lilly's café on the way over?" he asks, the suck-up.

"Why, that sounds wonderful. We'll look forward to it," she says, giving him a hug and pulling my dad inside the house. "We'll leave you two to say a proper goodnight."

My dad sends us both an apologetic look and lets her drag him into the house while I turn to Lucas, my face as bright as a beet-root.

"I'm SO sorry about that. All of that," I say, waving to where my parents have just disappeared. "I'm mortified."

Lucas pulls me close to him, linking his arms loosely behind my back, and smiles down at me.

"What are you doing?" I ask, confused.

"I'm pretty sure your mum is watching through the curtains," he says. "No, don't look. It'll be too obvious."

I groan and place my head on his chest, forgetting myself for the moment. "How will I ever repay you for tonight and tomorrow? My mum has been frightful."

"She's fine, you're fine," he says, his lips next to my ear. "It's been fun."

I look up into his blue eyes, which look darker and more soulful in this dim light, and give him a smile filled with doubt. "If that's the case, you need to get out more," I say.

Lucas throws his head back and laughs, causing me to laugh along with him. And just like that, I feel the tension from the evening dissipate.

"I'd better go," he says now, not making any move to let go of me.

"Sure," I reply, remaining still in his arms.

He looks down at me, his eyes focused on my lips and with a stifled groan, he steps back.

"Good night, Ames," he says, his voice a little hoarse. "I'll see you tomorrow."

I watch him leave, my heart heavy and light at the same time, and I think that I'd better get those guards back in place. Otherwise, neither I nor my heart will survive this weekend in one piece.

CHAPTER 20

THE NEXT MORNING, I GET the pleasure of hearing Mum rave about Lucas for several hours as we go shopping for shoes to match her new dresses.

"And he's so attentive to you, Amy. He could barely take his eyes off you the whole night," she tells me for the fifteenth time.

"I know, Mum, he's great," I tell her without enthusiasm.

"Did you see the way he spoke about staying here in Melbourne? Like you are the reason he wants to stay?"

"Calm down. We've only been together a few weeks," I say, trying to rein in her excitement. "It's all still very new."

"Mark my words, Amy Loo. That man is already in love with you!"

I groan out loud at this and attempt to distract Mum with the pretty shoe store in front of us. As she tries on a variety of shoes in many colours, I reflect on the fact that both Mum and Lilly are convinced Lucas is in love with me. I'm going to need him to dial it back at afternoon tea later today, or else our "break up" may overshadow the wedding altogether.

"What do you think? Is this the right colour to match my party dress?" Mum asks, calling my attention back to her.

"It's perfect!"

"Great, I'll get it. Now let's pick up something yummy to go with the treats Lucas is bringing to afternoon tea."

Mum purchases the shoes and then we spend the next thirty minutes choosing the perfect tea for Lucas to drink. Because, according to Diane Harlow, Lucas deserves the very best.

After we get back from shopping, my parents leave to spend some time with Lilly, Oliver and Snickers, and I retire to my room with a book, desperate for some downtime. And some time away from thinking about Lucas. I start reading my novel, one that I've been looking forward to reading for ages, only to get distracted by thoughts of Lucas. Lucas touching my hair, Lucas kissing my neck, Lucas holding me in his arms. And I force myself to examine the feelings I experience every time I'm around him. Have I been fooling myself this entire time, thinking that I just have a small crush on him? When we first met, I knew I could fall in love with him, even while we were fighting every day. And after that night together, I was pretty sure I was in love with him. But that all died when he left, didn't it?

I force myself to get up out of bed and do something to stop these thoughts from rolling around in my mind. With reading not holding my attention, I go to the living room and turn on the TV, only to find myself face to face with *Pride and Prejudice.* The same—now infamous—movie from the night Lucas and I decided to be friends. Is this the universe giving me a sign? That I should be happy to just be friends with Lucas? Or is it telling me to pursue him like he is my Mr Darcy? I sigh and turn off the TV, thinking that, in fact, this is no sign at all, except that this movie is caught in my Netflix algorithm. Distraction ideas abandoned, I decide to get ready for the upcoming afternoon tea with Lucas. Our last outing as a "couple." Why does that thought make me feel so sad?

He arrives just after three p.m., still wearing his scrubs and carrying a box of cookies and brownies from Lilly's bakery.

"Sorry, I didn't have time to change. It was a crazy day at the hospital today," he says, handing the treats to my mum and leaning over to kiss me like it's the most natural thing in the world.

My lips tingle from the slight brush of his, and I have to turn away so he won't see my cheeks flaming red.

"That's OK," Mum reassures him. "Why don't you take a shower in Amy's bathroom? We can wait for you," she adds.

Lucas and I look at each other, caught in this lie, not knowing how to extricate ourselves from it delicately.

"Um, do you have anything to change into?" I ask, feeling all sorts of uncomfortable.

"I have my clothes in the car, but I'm happy to stay in my scrubs. It's fine," he says, trying to give us an out.

"Nonsense. You'll feel much better once you've freshened up," she insists, looking at us like we're behaving weirdly, which we *are* for a couple who have no doubt used each other's bathrooms before.

"Ok, that sounds great," Lucas concedes, going to his car to get his bag.

Mum grabs my arm while I stand there looking at the space he left behind and says, "There's no need to be uncomfortable about this Amy. Your father and I are well aware that Lucas would have stayed over and used your shower before. We're all grown-ups here."

I grit my teeth and attempt to smile at my parents, noting that my dad does not look at all comfortable with this situation. "Thanks, Mum. Lucas needs a fresh towel to use. I'll go and get him one."

I all but run out of the room, bumping into Lucas as he reenters the house.

"I'm so sorry about this," I say, hanging my head and feeling miserable.

"Ames, it's fine. I'm actually happy to have a shower and get out of these scrubs. You won't believe the cases we had in the ER today."

Lucas fills me in on one of the more gruesome patient stories from this morning as I guide us to the bathroom.

"So, he just kept sawing through the wood and chopped off two of his fingers in the process?" I ask in dismay as we enter the bathroom. I give Lucas a towel and, still distracted by the story he's told me, I just stand there. Lucas doesn't seem to mind, and in a swift motion has his top off, standing in front of me in all his naked chest glory.

"Oh, sorry!" I say, coming out of my staring stupor as I notice him smirking at me. "I'll leave you to it," I add, forcing myself to walk out of the bathroom and away from his wonderful nakedness. "Enjoy!" I yell back at him as I leave like a giant dork. Today is not a good day.

When the freshly washed Lucas emerges from the shower, smelling like my minty soap, we sit down to afternoon tea at my small kitchen table. Mum makes a pot of tea, Lucas's favourite apparently, and keeps up a constant stream of small talk.

"Are you looking forward to the wedding?" my dad asks, speaking up for the first time this afternoon and dropping a bomb at the same time.

Lucas's eyes dart to mine while I furiously think of a suitable answer. Of course, he isn't looking forward to the wedding because he won't be attending the wedding. This fake relationship is ending in T-minus two hours.

"Of course he is, Tom." Mum saves us from answering.

We both nod along, avoiding any confirmation of this, while Lucas expertly changes the subject. "Are you two driving back home tonight?"

"Yes, we'll leave soon. It's always sad to leave the kids," she says, still referring to us like we're teenagers. "But I feel better knowing that Amy has you to look after her now."

I look at Lucas who is gazing back at me, an undecipherable expression on his face. "You're right, Di. She does have me now."

I blush and tear my eyes away from his, only to have them go right back without my permission.

"That's good to hear. And before we leave you two lovebirds alone, I'm just dying to know. What drew you to our Amy?" Mum says, completing my utter embarrassment quota for the day.

"You can't ask him that," I squeal, dying a little inside. "Ignore her," I beg Lucas, sending death stares in her direction.

Lucas gives me his signature grin, the one that's filled with confidence and makes my knees weak.

"It's a fair enough question for your mum to ask, Ames," he says, looking at my parents. "There are so many things that had me wanting to be with Amy. I love how passionate she is about her job, the way she cares and advocates for her patients. I love how she challenges me and doesn't back down from a fight, even if she's wrong," he adds, making my parents laugh. "Your daughter is so smart. It must be from all the books she reads, and the way her mind works constantly has me on my toes. She's kind and compassionate. She's a wonderful friend. And she's obviously beautiful. I could go on and on about all the things I love about her, but I wouldn't want her head to grow too big," he finishes, sending a smirk in my direction.

My parents stare at him with their mouths agape, while I am shocked into silence. *Did he just use the word* love *several times in that lovely little monologue?* I think. Or is it just that he had expected that sort of question and came prepared? He's so much better at this than I am.

"That's so nice to hear, Lucas," my mum finally finds her voice to say. "We obviously think Amy is pretty special, so it's good to know that her boyfriend feels the same way."

Lucas takes my hand in his and kisses my knuckles, gently rubbing his lips back and forth and causing goosebumps to spring up all along my arm.

"I think she's more than special," he replies in a soft voice, his eyes looking into mine. I swallow hard and cannot force myself to look away.

My dad clears his throat loudly, breaking the mood, making me wonder how long the two of us have been sitting here, just staring at each other.

"Di, we'd better get going. I'd like to get home by dinner time."

My parents excuse themselves to pack their stuff, leaving Lucas and me in a mess of muddled emotions. Well, OK, leaving *me* in this mess. I don't know what Lucas is feeling right now.

"That went well," he says, leaning back and helping himself to another brownie.

"Yes, you were amazing. Have you ever thought of a career in movies or television?" I ask, only half joking, trying to find out if he had been pretending when he said all that stuff about me.

"It was easy," he tells me.

"I'm glad you think so. It's been awful lying to my parents. I've been a sweaty mess all weekend."

Lucas gives me a long look and nods. "I didn't enjoy that part, but I enjoyed meeting your parents. And spending time with Lilly and Oliver. You are surrounded by great people, Amy."

I take a second to revel in pride at his observation before getting back to the problem at hand. Has he been pretending to care about me? Has any of this been real?

"So, you think I'm pretty amazing, hey?" I whisper to him, trying to test the waters.

Lucas gives me another one of his long looks. "I don't think I've ever hidden how amazing I think you are," he says in a low voice, standing up and tidying the kitchen table, effectively avoiding my eyes.

"OK, ummm," I reply, unsure of where to go from here. Is it time for me to just be honest and tell him how amazing I think he is as well? Just as I'm gathering up the nerve to start my monologue, my ode to Lucas if you will, my mum chooses this moment to ruin our moment.

"Lucas, dear, it's been lovely to meet you. I can't wait to see you at the wedding." She gives him a brief hug and then leaves us to it. I stand in silence and watch Lucas, trying to see where his head is at.

"I guess I'd better get going," he says, not moving...waiting for me to do something? "I'll see you at the hospital?" he adds when I appear to be rendered mute.

I nod and follow him out of the front door and to his car.

"I cannot thank you enough for what you've done for me this weekend," I finally find the words to say.

Lucas smiles and leans down to press another soft kiss on my lips. "It's been my pleasure to be your boyfriend, Amy. My absolute pleasure. Let's meet up and talk one day soon," he says, perhaps leaving the door open for us to get together and clarify what might be going on between us.

And with that, he gets in his car and drives away, leaving me to press my fingers to my lips and sigh. It was beyond a pleasure to be Lucas's girlfriend, and maybe one day soon I will get to do it again and it won't just be pretend.

CHAPTER 21

Two weeks after the weekend of fake dating, I'm at home getting both myself and Lilly ready for her bachelorette party. I've spent the last fortnight organising the best night out for Lilly and as such have had little time to focus on my love life. At work, Lucas and I have kept missing each other, and each time there has been even half a chance to have a proper conversation about "us," people asking us to do our jobs has interrupted us. The nerve of them. In the times when I haven't been working, I've been chatting with Madi and Sammi and we have a bachelorette party to remember—or forget—planned. We're starting with a party bus taking us to three of the trendiest bars in the city, ending at our favourite karaoke spot where we're meeting up with Oliver and his bachelor party. Apparently, Lilly and Oliver cannot spend one night apart, so this is the compromise. I was fine with it until I learnt that Oliver, in a moment of confusion, invited my "boyfriend" Lucas to attend his party, and so now I face the reality of seeing him later tonight, in the presence of alcohol. Is this a good opportunity to figure out if we can be something more than friends?

"Do I have to wear this?" Lilly whines from next to me, drawing me out of my anxious thoughts.

I look at Lilly, who's wearing a pale pink figure-hugging dress that looks amazing on her hourglass figure, and nod. "Yes! You're the bride; this is your night. You cannot wear jeans and sneakers!"

She gives me a forlorn look and forces her feet into a pair of heels. "If this is my night, then why can't I wear what I want?" she asks—a very reasonable question.

"Because we live in a society, Lilly, where we often have to get dressed up in uncomfortable clothes and leave the house to have some fun," I lecture her, finishing her make-up. "Here, have a shot of tequila. A few of these and you won't be feeling your feet anymore."

She smiles at me as we both take a shot of tequila, wincing as the alcohol burns its way down our throats.

"That's the spirit," I say, my eyes still watering a little. "Let me fix my hair and then we'll be ready to go."

"Have I told you how hot you look tonight?" Lilly asks, always my biggest cheerleader.

I look at myself in the mirror and have to admit that I have put together a pretty decent look for the evening. My dress is also figure-hugging, black with a high neck and long sleeves, a nod to the cooler May Melbourne weather. The hero of the dress, though, is the bare back, which I highlight by putting my hair up in a sleek, high ponytail. The hemline stops mid-thigh and I finish the look off with a pair of sky-high gold heels. In this outfit, I feel sexy and sophisticated.

"I think I hear Madi and Sammi," Lilly says, getting up to answer the door, wobbling a bit on her heels.

I follow behind her, picking up my small gold handbag as I go, and am greeted by the sounds of squealing as she lets the girls in. They come armed with a "Bride to Be" sash and a tiara for Lilly. She looks mortified as we decorate her. It's amazing.

"OK, ladies. One more shot of tequila for the road," I say, handing out four shot glasses. We all down the drinks and head outside to be greeted by a hot-pink party bus filled with Lilly's friends. With the music already pumping, and the girls hanging out of the windows waving madly at us, we know we're in for a fantastic night ahead.

Two hours later, we're at bar stop number three. So far, we've had many cocktails at the first stop, and many shots at bar number two. And here, at the third stop, we seem to have embraced being straight-up rowdy.

"To the bride! We love you so much!" Sammi cheers as we slam down another shot of tequila. These latest shots are going down too smoothly, which speaks to how drunk we are.

"Lilly! I can't wait to be your sister!" I yell, pulling her in for a drunken hug.

"I can't wait either! And I can't believe I'm getting married," she slurs in reply, linking her arm through mine and squeezing me tight. "I feel so grown up! Oh look, they're dancing on the bar! Let's go do that!" Lilly, "the grown-up," pulls us all up on the bar-top, where we attempt to dance and not fall to our deaths. It's great fun!

A thousand drinks later, after we've survived the balancing act on the bar tables, we arrive at the Karaoke King Bar, ready to sing. "We're doing 'Single Ladies' by Beyonce," Madi yells, grabbing Sammi to join her on stage. I watch as the two of them sing—yell—the words, calling all the single ladies to the dance floor, laughing at their attempts at matching choreography.

"We're up next," Lilly shouts in my ear, her volume control getting worse with each consecutive drink. "Come on, Ames!"

I'm right behind her, feeling emboldened by all the alcohol. Plus, I love karaoke. When we get on stage and I hear the first notes of the song that Lilly chose for us, I give her a big smile. Taylor Swift. We grab the microphone and start belting out the lines to one of our favourite ever single-girl song.

"We are never, ever getting back together," I yell, not even attempting to sing in tune, hugging Lilly to my side. "Like ever!" We laugh in unison. I look out into the crowd and see him. Lucas. Leaning against the wall, smiling his delicious smile at me, and I can't find it in me to be embarrassed. The look that he's giving me says he's enjoying what he's watching.

The song ends to a round of applause, though they may be applauding us getting off the stage, and Lilly and I make a big show of curtseying and bowing, before reluctantly joining our friends. Lilly is immediately swept up into Oliver's arms, the two of them kissing like they haven't seen each other in weeks, rather than the hours they've been apart. I give them some privacy and head to the bar. Time for another drink.

At the bar, I order myself another cocktail and while I'm waiting for the concoction to be made, I feel a hand on my back. I turn to see a good-looking guy smiling at me.

"You were great up there," he lies, giving me a long look up and down.

"Thanks, but I know you're lying," I laugh up at him.

"Not at all." He moves closer into my personal space, touching my hip, making me feel uncomfortable.

"Um, right then," I say, grabbing my drink and going to move away. The stranger steps even closer, crowding me back into the bar, blocking my exit.

"I'm Nate, by the way. Do you want to dance?" he asks, his face too close to mine.

"Hey, babe. Sorry I'm late." I feel an arm wrap around me, pulling me away from the handsy guy and into a safe, warm chest. Lucas. I turn to see him glaring at the man in front of me while tucking me even closer to him.

"That's alright," I say. "Let's go dance." I pull the angry-looking Lucas away to the dance floor, where he follows, his jaw clenched in displeasure.

"Who was that?" he asks as we step onto the dance floor, his eyes still focused on the man at the bar.

"No one," I tell him. "He just wanted to dance with me."

Lucas finally looks down at me. His eyes heated as they travel the length of my body, lingering on the short hemline of my dress.

"Well, we can't blame him for wanting that. You look amazing, Ames," he whispers into my ear, drawing me closer to him. We both start moving slowly to the upbeat music, oblivious to the rowdy crowd surrounding us.

"You do too," I tell him—because he does. Every woman in the bar tonight is looking at him hungrily. "You smell good, too," I whisper, leaning my face close to his neck.

"We really need to talk," he says into my ear.

"I know," I reply, snuggling in closer to him, not wanting to talk at all.

Lucas groans deep in his throat and roughly pulls me flush against his body, resting his forehead on mine.

"It's been too long," he whispers.

"Since what?" I ask, looking up at him.

"This."

Lucas's lips crash onto mine, kissing me with so much intensity it steals my breath away. After the briefest moment, I respond, kissing him back with all the emotion I've been feeling for the past month, years. He nibbles on my lips, urging them to open, and then assaults me with his tongue. The kiss is so sensual that I let out an involuntary whimper, causing him to deepen the kiss further. We kiss for what feels like hours, not coming up for air, not wanting to let this moment go. I feel his warm hands on my bare back, pulling me even closer as I part my legs to accommodate him and run my hands through his hair. I know where this is going—

"Amy?! Where are you?" Lilly's voice screeches from up on the stage, her mouth too close to the microphone, causing it to let out an ear-splitting sound.

Lucas and I jump apart, my fingers coming up to touch my swollen lips while I look around, confused. Where am I again?

"Amy? Come up here, it's time to siinnngg again," she yells.

I look at Lucas, who is breathing heavily, and reluctantly take a step away from him.

"I'd better get up there," I tell him, my voice coming out in a hoarse whisper. He nods at me, his cheeks still flushed with desire.

"You go. I'll be here waiting."

I stumble away from him, my knees still weak from that earth-shattering kiss, and make my way onto the stage where Lilly, Madi and Sami are waiting for me. The first few notes of "Wannabe" by the Spice Girls begin and I'm swept up in performing it all, dancing and singing along in our own girl group. Once we've finished singing "zig-a-zig ah," we hop off stage to more applause and many more drinks. And then, the night becomes a bit of a blur. I'm aware of Lucas beside me or behind me, holding me close, throughout the rest of the evening. I know there's more dancing and more kissing. And more drinking. And that's where things get even more fuzzy. I can't be sure, but I may have fallen over at some stage and then there was the feeling of being carried while waving goodbye to my friends, before it goes dark.

"Morning, sunshine," a familiar male voice says softly from beside me. I pry one eyelid open and wince as the light attacks my eyeballs. I put a hand out to feel the face of the voice next to me. Lucas. No! I groan and put the pillow over my head.

"Mhakdndpp," I mumble.

"What was that?" he asks, laughing at me.

"Imehoanbs," I clarify.

Lucas takes the pillow off my head, and using his fingers, he turns my face toward his.

"You need to use your words properly, Ames. How are you feeling?"

"Dying," I force through lips that are as dry as the Sahara.

"What can I do to help?" he asks, running a gentle hand over my hair, a soothing motion on my pounding headache.

"Cheeseburger, fries, coke. Please," I say, opening one eye to plead with him.

He gives me a dubious look. "Really? All that grease will not help your hangover."

I point my finger to what I assume is the doorway and tell him in a serious voice, "It's the only way I can get through this."

I must sound so miserable that Lucas takes pity on me. He rolls over and, after giving me the softest kiss on the cheek, tells me he'll be back with my order as soon as possible.

"Make it two cheeseburgers," I yell after him as he's leaving, causing myself to grimace at the sound of my own loud voice.

After he's gone, I roll over onto my back and try to take stock of the situation. I'm obviously in Lucas's bed. I feel under the covers to find that I'm no longer in my sexy black dress from last night, and upon further inspection, it would seem that I'm wearing one of his T-shirts. It has "University of London" written on the front of it and is a delightful shade of light green. I decide on the spot that it's mine now.

OK, I know where I am, but how did I get here? A variety of images flash through my mind, including the mind-blowing kiss (kisses?) that Lucas and I shared. In addition to some truly horrendous karaoke singing and many, many shots of tequila. That would explain the sandpaper mouth and the throbbing headache.

I grab my phone when I hear it ping and see several text messages from Lilly. Checking up on me, cursing me for allowing her to drink so much, and questioning "*What was with all the kissing?*" According to the messages from Oliver, I was so embarrassingly intoxicated (his words, not mine), they decided it was for the best that Lucas take me home. Oliver now thinks that Lucas is a stand-up guy and that I should not "mess that up again." Thanks, big brother.

With my head feeling heavy, I force myself to sit up and wait for the room to stop spinning. I can only imagine how bad I look right now! With the need to pee stronger than the need to bury my head back under the covers, I tentatively get out of bed and stand up. With extra care, I make my way out of the bedroom in search of the bathroom and walk straight into the muscular form of Lucas's roommate.

"Amy?" the roommate speaks.

I look up to see Daniel standing in front of me, a look of amusement on his face.

"Hey, Daniel," I say, attempting to pull down the hem of the T-shirt to cover more of my bare thighs. "I'm looking for the bathroom?"

He gives me a small smirk and nods his head toward the door next to him. "It's just through there."

"Thanks!" I say, rushing past him and closing the door behind me.

Once inside, I take a moment to stare at myself in the mirror in horror, noting my bloodshot eyes and rumpled hair. What a mess! After peeing for about an hour straight, I use whatever I can in the boys' bathroom—which isn't much—to fix the damage from last night. I swirl mouthwash around to erase the bitter aftertaste of tequila—yuck—while using a face cloth to wipe away the make-up smeared all over my face. What an absolute disaster. I cannot believe I let Lucas see me like this.

With a defeated sigh, I leave the bathroom and see him entering the house, a bag of takeout in his hands. The smell of fried food makes my mouth water and I promptly forget my mattered hair and face, racing toward him.

"Gimme!" I say, grabbing for the bag.

Lucas laughs at me, his eyes travelling all over my body, pausing on his T-shirt.

"You should only wear my clothes from now onwards," he shocks me by saying, his voice taking on a gravelly tone.

I flush bright red and feel myself swoon a bit. "Mhmm," I manage to say, following him and the hangover cure into the kitchen.

Once we sit down, I grab the food, taking a huge bite out of my cheeseburger while simultaneously shoving a handful of fries into my mouth. So good! With a big slurp of drink and another two bites, I feel a little better and sit back with a sigh.

"Feeling better?" Lucas asks, while sipping on his cup of coffee, looking no worse for wear after a night out drinking.

"Umm, yes. Sorry about last night," I mumble, looking down at the fries that I'm about the devour. Oh, the salty goodness. "And thanks for looking after me. I don't remember much, but I'm thinking it wasn't pretty."

Lucas smiles at me. "You're always pretty, Amy," he says, causing my heart to flutter. "And I love taking care of you."

I pause in the process of chewing to stare at him. This beautiful man who always says the right thing.

"Lucas—"

"Hey, man." Daniel chooses that moment to enter the room. "Oops, sorry," he says, looking between the two of us. "I didn't mean to interrupt."

I watch as the two of them exchange a silent look with some unspoken communication between them.

"No, you aren't interrupting, Dan. In fact, I probably should get going. I have to work later tonight, and I need to get myself together."

Daniel makes an apologetic face at Lucas—weird—and waves goodbye, leaving us alone again.

"I'll drive you home," he says with a resigned sigh. "But first, you need some pants."

I follow him to his room, my sense of embarrassment going up several notches, and gather up my clothes, trying all the while to not imagine Lucas undressing me last night. The thought of that makes my whole body hot and bothered.

"Here, these have a drawstring, you should be able to make them fit."

I take the shorts from Lucas and after pulling them on and tightening the drawstring, I turn to see him watching, a grin on his face.

"Shut up!" I tell him, knowing just how ridiculous I must look.

"You look adorable," he says, coming up to me and pressing a kiss on my forehead. "Come on, let's get you home."

On the short drive back to my place, we sit in silence. The events of last night are sitting heavily between us with so much left unspoken. After he drops me at my front door with yet another delightful little kiss, this time on my cheek, he finally says, "Amy, we really need to talk."

I nod. "Yes, maybe tomorrow? When there isn't a jackhammer in my head?"

Lucas gives me an indulgent smile and agrees. "Tomorrow, after work. Let's go out for dinner?"

Is this a date? I think, excited and nervous at the same time.

"Sounds good. Let's do that."

I watch as he drives away and think this date will be the perfect time to lay all my cards on the table and let him know how I feel. I just have to hope to god that he feels the same way, too.

CHAPTER 22

LATER THAT DAY, AFTER A little nanna nap and several large cups of coffee, I drag myself out of my car and into the hospital to start my shift. When I had planned Lilly's bachelorette party, I hadn't expected a hangover to beat all hangovers, but here I am, feeling very worse for wear, about to start an eight-hour night shift.

"Hey Tim," I say to the on-duty nurse, whose shift I'm taking over. "Anything I need to know from today?"

Tim gives me a once-over look, hiding a quick smile behind his hands, before taking out a handful of charts and walking me through handover. *That was weird,* I think after we're done. Maybe I still smell of alcohol? I try subtly to smell my underarms as I go to treat my first patient, noticing a few of the other staff members glancing my way and smirking. One of the consultant doctors whispers to his colleague behind his hands as I walk past, causing me to wonder whether I'd put scrubs on back to front or something.

I shrug, not knowing what to make of the strange behaviour of my colleagues and then get back to work. The emergency room is already heaving with patients, and I know this'll get worse as the night gets older. I gear myself up for a long evening ahead and wishing, not for the first time, that I hadn't had so much to drink last night.

The next morning, as I prepare for another shift at the hospital, I think about the way a few of my workmates behaved yesterday. After the initial smirking and some laughing, things seemed to settle down, but I couldn't shake the feeling that they were all talking about me. The only upside is that I'm feeling so much better today and I have a date with Lucas to look forward to.

"Hey, Ames." Jamie greets me as I enter the office to sign in. "Are you OK?"

I give him a bemused look while I log on to the computer. "Sure, I'm fine. Why?" I ask, distracted, trying to remember my password. *Why do they make us change it so often?*

"Well, because of the video that's been circulating. I thought it may have upset you," he says, his voice uncharacteristically serious.

I stop what I am doing and look up at him. "What video?"

Jamie's face turns a shade of pink and his mouth gapes open a little. "You haven't seen it?"

"Seen what?" I demand, a frisson of worry creeping down my spine. What's he talking about? "Jamie, what are you talking about?"

He sighs and takes his phone out of his pocket. Logging into his Facebook account, he clicks on a link and a loud video begins to play. I grab the phone from him to look. There on the screen, in what looks like high-definition footage, is me and Lucas in a very passionate embrace. At the karaoke bar, by the sounds of the horrible singing in the background. Kissing. Locked in each other's arms, oblivious to the world around us. And it doesn't stop there, there's more. Next, I'm on stage singing, and then more footage of me kissing Lucas, and then Lucas has me swung over his shoulder, his arms locked around my thighs, carrying me out of the bar while I'm blowing kisses to everyone around me. Who took this video?

"How did this happen?" I ask, my hands shaking.

"From what I can decipher, a few of your friends posted videos from the night on their socials, and someone on the internet has taken the time to crop these bits of you into one video."

"This is awful," I say, looking at the screen paused on the image of me slung over Lucas's shoulder.

"It's not so bad," Jamie says, noting the horror on my face. "You just look like someone who had a great night out."

"I look like someone who was mauling the face of a co-worker. Who also carried me out like we were going to have sex or something." I feel my face getting hotter as I watch it again.

"Did you? Have sex?" Jamie asks, missing the point.

"No! He just...took me home and helped me to bed."

"Hmmm, shame. Because it really looked like he was carrying you caveman-style to have his way with you."

I groan as he says this. "Not helping, Jamie. Do you think everyone has seen this? Is that why people have been acting so strange around me?"

He avoids my eyes and gives a little shrug. "I think some people may have seen it..."

"Jamie. Tell me!"

"It somehow made its way onto the ER Facebook group page. I'm surprised you didn't see it on there."

"I'm not on Facebook, you know that. Does that mean, like, everyone has seen it?" I look at him, the idea of this video circulating around the department making me want to throw up.

"It would appear so, if some of these comments are anything to go by."

"Comments?" I ask, taking the phone from him again and having another look. "Oh my god. This is worse than I thought."

I read a few of the first comments, some are light-hearted but most mean-spirited. Many anonymous users mention the words *easy* and *messy* or *SLUT*?

"Someone called me a slut? From that video?" I ask Jamie, my voice trembling with emotion. Who would say that about someone online?

"Don't worry about it, Ames," Jamie says, pulling me in for a hug. "It's a story on social media today that will be forgotten by tomorrow. It's nothing."

"It's not nothing. You know what I went through at CMH, what happened with me and James. I can't handle anything like that following me around here."

"But you said nothing happened. So, we wait for the story to die down and then we move on," Jamie tells me with his voice of reason, making me feel slightly better.

"You think so?" I ask as my phone beeps next to me. I pick it up and see an email from Human Resources requesting to meet with me and Hector in an hour. My stomach drops and I show the screen to Jamie. This could only be about one thing.

"It'll be fine," he says again after reading the email, sounding a lot less confident now. "Don't jump to any conclusions."

I nod but cannot shake the dread I'm feeling inside. What have I done?

An hour later, I'm sitting in Hector's office with Janine from HR sitting off to the side. I wipe my sweaty palms on my scrubs in front of me and try to project a picture of serene confidence. I'm a person with nothing to hide. I have done nothing wrong.

"Do you know why I've called you in here today, Ms Harlow?" Hector asks now, looking at me from over his glasses.

"I'm not sure?" I answer.

"Are you aware of the video that is circulating on the Facebook? It shows you in a compromising position with Dr Mancini," he says, his face blushing brightly.

"Uh, yes. I saw the video. I'm not sure where it came from, or who recorded it. It's very embarrassing. We were at my best friend's bachelorette party and..." I trail off, unsure what they want me to say.

"Quite a few people in the hospital have seen the video, and many of these people have raised concerns about it. Well, about you."

I look at Hector with confusion. Why would that video of me make the people I work with uncomfortable?

"I'm not sure what you mean, Hector? It's not like I was at work at the time. It was after hours."

"But you were with a colleague, and you were...kissing..."

I look at Janine, who is shifting with discomfort in her seat, and seek to understand where he's going with this.

"Hector, what's the actual concern here?"

He clears his throat, also looking very uncomfortable while Janine takes over.

"Are you aware that Dr Mancini is on the hiring committee and will decide whether you get the promotion for Chief Nursing Officer?" she says, dropping a bomb on me. How did I not know this?

"No," I stammer, feeling my face going pale as the blood drains from there down to my toes. "I wasn't aware."

"And so, with this video thing making the rounds, it's going to cause people to question any decision we make about future career prospects," Hector says.

I look at him with dismay. After working here diligently for years, with all the unpaid overtime and volunteer upskilling I do, he's telling me that this video has the power to derail it all.

"I would hope that the hospital could distinguish my professional life from my personal life," I tell him, finding my voice and using it firmly. This is bullshit. "I would also hope that if Lucas, I mean Dr Mancini, is on the committee, that a group of intelligent people like yourselves could find a way to work around it. And finally, I would have thought the people I've worked beside every day for the past four years would agree that I'm the best person for this promotion, video or no video." My chest is heaving with emotion as I finish up.

Hector stares at me, a little shocked at my outburst, before he nods. "I agree, Ms Harlow. And that is the way the world should work. I'm just hoping it is the case for you."

I get up, clearly having been dismissed, and walk out of the office on shaky legs. As soon as I've rounded the corner, I lean back against the wall and sink to the floor. How had I let this happen again? How had I let my feelings for a man potentially derail everything I have worked so hard for?

"Amy?"

I look up to see Lucas standing above me, his face filled with concern. "Jamie told me about your meeting with Hector and HR. What happened?"

He sits down on the floor next to me, going to put his arm around my shoulder before I pull away, forcing him to shift away from me slightly.

"Oh, nothing much," I tell him, my voice bitter. "It would seem that me kissing you is going to ruin my career."

"What?" he says, shocked.

"Have you seen the video?" Lucas nods. "Well, apparently, so has everyone in the hospital, too. And some think that makes me unfit to be Chief Nursing Officer."

Lucas's face darkens with anger and he gets up to pace in front of me.

"That's complete bullshit, Ames. And you know it. Who do I need to talk to?"

I look at him, feeling so defeated. He can't fix this for me, he's part of the problem.

"Why didn't you tell me you're on the hiring committee for my promotion?"

Lucas stops pacing and looks down at me. "I was going to take myself off the board once I knew what we were. Officially. I didn't anticipate that bloody video."

"Well, it's too late now. The damage is done. I've let some stupid kisses ruin everything I have worked so hard for."

Lucas gives me an injured look, causing me to swallow hard and look away from him.

"Stupid kisses?" he rasps.

I shake my head, not wanting to go into any of this. My only thoughts now are on damage control.

"I can't do this." I stand up and move away from him before he grabs my arm, forcing me to turn around and look at him.

"Can't do what, Amy?" he asks me, raising his voice slightly.

"You," I throw at him. "Any of this. I can't do this again."

"Do what again?" he asks, sounding exasperated. "Why don't we just go out to dinner as we'd planned and talk about it? We can sort this out. I can speak to Hector. I can fix this."

"Don't do anything!" I say sharply, not wanting him to speak on my behalf. Not wanting him near anything to do with my career. "The damage is done. You speaking up for me will only make this worse."

"So, what then? You won't even take the time to try to work this out? That's it? It's done? We're done?"

I look at Lucas, at his beautiful blue eyes and his perfect mouth, and almost back down. But then I see a group of nurses at the end of the corridor watching us and whispering, and I'm reminded of what's at stake here.

I steel myself for the lie I know I need to tell. "There won't be a dinner date tonight, Lucas. And there is no we." And with that, I force myself to walk away from the man I love to protect a career that I think I love even more.

CHAPTER 23

Lucas

I'M SITTING IN THE DARKENED living room, staring at a blank TV, when Daniel finds me later that afternoon.

"Hey man," he says from the doorway. "You don't look so good."

He comes further into the room and sits in the armchair across from me, his head tilted in confusion.

"When you left this morning, you looked like a man with the world at his feet. What happened?"

I take a sip of my now lukewarm beer and shrug. I don't know what happened.

"Don't know, Dan. I went to work, you know, excited to be going out for dinner tonight. On a proper date. A chance to tell her how I feel, at last." He nods for me to continue. "And then some stuff went down with her boss and HR about our relationship and she bolted. Told me we were 'nothing' and walked away." Even saying it now is causing a sharp pain in my chest. I rub at it, watching Daniel's face scrunch with sympathy.

"That's rough. I thought after seeing her here the other night that you two were finally going to sort your stuff out."

"Hmmm," I mumble, not wanting to talk about it anymore. Not wanting to think about it. I've been thinking about and hurting over Amy for too long. "Maybe it's time I just accept that she doesn't want to be with me. She's been pulling away from me since the moment we met. I had thought that if we tried to be friends that we could perhaps naturally grow into something more. Now I'm thinking that it's time to let her go."

Daniel nods as he takes in what I'm saying. "That sounds reasonable. But..." He trails off.

"But what?"

"Well, you haven't been able to get over her for the past two years. From what you have told me, she's the love of your life. What's different this time?"

I think about it. About the look on Amy's face when she walked away from me. This time there is no misunderstanding standing between us. She's deliberately cutting things off between us, and I need to respect it. I need to be done with it. With her.

"She's made her position very clear. I have to let her go."

I look at Daniel and then have to look away due to what I see on his face.

"Want to get some pizza and watch the footy?" he asks in his very "Australian male" way. Apparently, Aussie Rules Football is the cure for everything.

"Sounds good. You order the pizza and I'll go pick it up."

As he leaves to place the order, I pick up my phone to scroll through Instagram, trying to keep my mind off Amy. I'm watching a cute dog video when a call comes through from an unknown number.

"Hello?" I ask, hoping it's not a spam call. I'm not in the mood.

"Lucas?" comes a familiar female voice.

"Yes?"

"It's Lilly," the voice says, sending shockwaves through me. Lilly is calling me? Is Amy OK?

"Amy's fine," she reassures me. "Well, she's not great, actually. That's why I'm calling you. I was wondering if you could meet with me? Just for five minutes?"

I pull my phone back to look at the screen, buying myself a moment to gather my thoughts. Why would Lilly want to meet with me?

"I know you don't owe Amy anything, but I need to tell you a few things. Maybe explain some stuff..." Lilly trails off, like she's questioning whether she should be speaking with me in the first place.

"When and where do you want to meet?" I say quickly, before she can back out of her offer.

"How about now? Can you come to my café?"

"I'm on my way," I tell her, hanging up and grabbing my shoes as I move toward the door.

"Dan, you'll need to get that pizza delivered. I'm going out."

Daniel pokes his out of the kitchen, giving me a puzzled look.

"I'll explain later. And I'll bring home some cookies," I yell, rushing out the door.

I arrive at Lilly's café less than ten minutes later, grateful that I live close by. When I park the car, I see her waiting for me out front, hair in a haphazard bun atop her head and chocolate smeared on her face.

"Hey, Lilly," I say, getting out of my car and walking toward her. I'm not sure what she sees on my face, but whatever it is, it causes her to pull me into a big, warm hug, offering me the comfort I didn't know I needed.

I let myself lean into it for a moment before pulling back and following her inside.

"I've just taken a batch of brownies out of the oven. We'll eat that with a big bowl of vanilla ice cream. And we'll talk," she says, spearing me with a look.

I nod. It's fine by me, I came here to talk. Once Lilly has plated up the dessert in front of us, she leans back and looks at me.

"I'll start by saying that Amy would kill me if she knew I was here with you. But I can't stand by and watch you both continue to make a mess of everything. You clearly need some outside help."

Agreeing with her, I nod and take a bite of the brownie, groaning as I do so.

"Good, hey?" she asks with a grin.

"So good," I agree.

"Now, Lucas, let me ask you this. Has Amy ever explained to you why she was so antagonistic toward you right from the start?"

"I always assumed it was because I was the new guy who came onto her turf and thought I knew better."

Lilly gives me a wry smile. "Well, that didn't help. But think back further. To the night you guys met. What did you say to make her run away from you?"

I take a second to recall, seeing the whole interaction in my mind as if it were yesterday. It was a pretty monumental day for me, after all.

"It was when I told her I was a doctor. Working in her hospital."

She nods. "Right. That was a trigger for her. Have you ever wondered why?"

"I didn't think about it too much. I was just so grateful to find her again after the two of you ran away. Is there something else I should know about?"

Lilly takes a deep breath and starts to explain what happened with Amy and James at her first job out of university. As I listen to the details, to what that jerk did to her when she was so young and vulnerable, I feel my hands clench in anger.

"When I think of what his wife did, coming in and calling Amy a slut in front of all her colleagues, it makes me so angry." Her cheeks flush as she recounts that part of the story. "If I ever see her, she had better watch out. James too, the arse-hat."

"You will need to get in line," I grind out between clenched teeth, so angry on Amy's behalf.

"Yes, well. You can imagine what seeing that video and reading those comments did to Amy today. Add in the conversation she had with that dinosaur Hector, and it absolutely shattered her. She's so protective of her career, so determined to never let a man derail it again. And now every fear of hers has come back to life. She's a mess."

The thought of Amy upset, alone and in pain, makes my chest hurt again. I rub at the familiar spot that's aching above my heart and ask Lilly the question I need to know the answer to.

"What does this mean for me? For me and Amy?" I know I sound desperate and pathetic, but I can't find it in me to care anymore.

She gives me a long, assessing look, taking her time to answer. "Lucas, you don't need to go into details with me, but do you care for Amy?"

"I love her," I say without a moment of hesitation.

She blinks at me, her face breaking into a wide smile. "I was hoping you would say that. What Amy needs right now is for you not to give up on her. She's hurting, she isn't thinking straight. Suddenly, everything that could have gone wrong has gone wrong, and she's retreating. She's pulling away, like she did when you went back to Florence."

I look back on that whole situation now with a new appreciation. Amy had to overcome so much emotional baggage just to be with me that night, and then for me to leave her for "another woman," it must have killed her.

I say this to Lilly, who nods along with me. "It did. Amy was a wreck for months after. She had finally let you in, and you turned out to be James 2.0." I go to argue, and she puts her hand up to stop me. "We know now that you were an innocent victim in all of this. In fact, she knows she hurt you. That her behaviour caused you pain. And she's been struggling with that since you came back."

"And yet, here we are again. How do I make this right?"

"You still want to make it right? Even after everything?"

I nod, surer of this than anything else in my life. "Amy is it for me. I need to try. One more time."

Another smile crosses Lilly's face, one filled with relief this time. "Good to know. I think I can help you out there. Well, somewhat..."

"Tell me, what can I do?"

"Amy has gotten herself convinced that her career is more important than anything else. You need to convince her that what you have together, what you feel for each other, is the most important thing."

"How do I do that?" I ask, eager for guidance.

"That...? I don't know. You'll need to figure it out for yourself. But I can give you some brownies for while you do it," she finishes, standing up to fill a takeaway container with all the treats.

I stand too, confused, but lighter at the same time.

"Lilly, do you think I have a chance? That Amy has genuine feelings for me?" I ask, feeling silly for asking, but so desperate for some sort of affirmation.

"She wouldn't be at home crying herself to sleep on her couch right now if she didn't have actual feelings for you, Lucas. Trust me, I think with some gentle encouragement, the two of you will be together in no time. For real this time."

I take the cardboard box filled with cookies and brownies from Lilly's hands and give her a grateful hug goodbye.

"Just remember, you were never here. We never met," she says as she ushers me out of the door. "And good luck, Lucas. I'm rooting for the two of you."

With a final wave to Lilly, I get back into my car and start driving home. I have an idea, a way to show Amy how I feel about her and now that I have a plan in place, I can't wait to get started. Amy had better watch out. I'm not giving up on us so easily.

CHAPTER 24

Amy

After the day from hell, I'm now sitting on the couch, crying and feeling very sorry for myself. With Snickers cuddled in close to my side, I bury my face in his fur, allowing him to cover my face with doggie kisses. I need the comfort. Lilly had just popped over to drop off a box of brownies and Snickers for the night. She says he's the perfect antidote for heartache, and so far, she hasn't been wrong. Lilly also gave me an enigmatic smile and a pep talk before she left, telling me she had a "feeling" that everything was going to work out. This new serene and optimistic version of Lilly is pissing me off.

Just as I'm pouring myself my second glass of wine for the evening, well aware that drinking my problems away is not the answer but not caring enough to do anything about it, I hear a knock at my front door. Snickers barks like crazy, running to the door to greet my visitor, while I trail behind him.

I open the door and am shocked to see Lucas standing there. He looks wrecked. His eyes are sad and tired, and his hair looks like he's run his hands through it too many times in the last few hours. I feel a big pang of guilt knowing I did this to him.

"Hi," I say, opening the door wider to let him in.

"Don't worry, I'm not here to stay. I just came over to give you this," he says, thrusting a small folder into my hands.

With shaky hands, I take it from him. "What is it?"

"They're all the emails I wrote to you while I was away. The ones you blocked and that bounced back to me. I printed them out."

With my cheeks flushed with shame, shaking my head, I go to give the folder back to him. "I don't deserve to read these," I say, my eyes filling with tears. I'm just so exhausted.

Lucas stops my hands. "Please read them. And if, after you've done so, you want to talk, you can call me. I do hope you call me," he finishes, walking backward away from me over to his car.

"Lucas—" I start, unsure of what to do in this moment.

"Just read them," he calls, before getting in his car and driving away with a little wave.

I walk back into the house, filling my glass with even more wine. With a brownie in one hand and Snickers cuddled into my side, I take a deep breath, open the folder, and start reading.

TO: amy.harlow@mercyhealth.com;
FROM: the.doc.mancini@gmail.com;
SUBJECT: Update

Dear Amy,

I'm so sorry about the way I behaved yesterday. You would have heard by now from Hector that my papa collapsed and was taken to the hospital. That phone call threw me off balance, and I couldn't gather my thoughts together and just tell you what was going on.

I'm sorry.

I just landed in Florence. It took forever to get here, and I've only just seen my papa. Turns out he had a stroke. He's about to go into surgery now, to clear the clot. The doctors here are hoping to get in before any permanent damage is done. As you well know, the first forty-eight hours after a stroke are the most crucial. I'm glad I could get here to see him before they put him under and that I can support Isabella and my mamma.

I tried to call you but it didn't go through. I'll try to sort out my international roaming. After I know more about what's happening here, I'll contact you again.

Our night together was very special to me. I need you to know that.

I'll be in touch.

Love,
Lucas

TO: amy.harlow@mercyhealth.com;
FROM: the.doc.mancini@gmail.com;
SUBJECT: Technical Difficulties?

Dear Amy,

The last email I sent you bounced back to me, which is weird because I'm pretty sure I typed your email address in correctly. Maybe you are having some technical issues on your end? I also can't get through to your phone, even though I can call Hector at the hospital just fine.

Hector told me he informed the staff of my situation and that I may need to be away for some time. Is that what you've heard?

Why haven't you tried to call me?

My papa's surgery went well and he's now in the ICU being monitored closely. We will know more once he wakes up, but we are hopeful he will pull through.

My sister and mamma are pretty stressed out, so I'm holding it together for us all. But Ames, between you and me, I'm scared. My papa is my hero, he's indestructible. So, to see him like this, hooked up to all these machines, it's hard.

I'm going to call you again. And I hope you get this. And I hope you reply.

Love,
Lucas

TO: amy.harlow@mercyhealth.com;
FROM: the.doc.mancini@gmail.com;
SUBJECT: What's going on?

Amy,

The last email bounced back again, and your phone is still not working. If we hadn't just spent the most magical night together, I would think you blocked me. But that makes no sense. Why would you do that?

I'm choosing to believe that you are experiencing apocalyptic-level technical issues and that I will hear from you any minute now.

My papa is out of the ICU and it looks like he may have some paralysis on his left side. He will need months of rehabilitation to walk properly again and to regain the use of his arm.

I may need to stay here for a bit longer.

I really need to talk to you. Please call me.

Love,
Lucas

TO: amy.harlow@mercyhealth.com;
FROM: the.doc.mancini@gmail.com;
SUBJECT:???

Amy,

The last three emails have bounced back and the last ten phone calls have gone unanswered. Are you blocking me?

What's going on?

Why are you doing this?

I know I didn't handle my departure well, but this? This reaction? I just don't understand.

Call me if you ever get this.

I'll be waiting.

Lucas

TO: amy.harlow@mercyhealth.com;
FROM: the.doc.mancini@gmail.com;
SUBJECT: Another update

Dear Amy,

After a month of calling with no response, I get the message. You don't want to hear from me. And yet here I am, emailing you like a fool.

I have always been a fool over you, Amy.

My papa is doing better. He has moved home with Mamma, and me and Isabella are taking turns helping with his rehabilitation. And I'm also helping run the deli.

I don't know when I will be able to come home. That's to you. You are my home.

I miss you.

Love,
Lucas

TO: amy.harlow@mercyhealth.com;
FROM: the.doc.mancini@gmail.com;
SUBJECT: That first night...

Dear Amy,

I know you won't read this, but I find I like writing to you. It makes me feel close to you, which is crazy because you clearly don't want to be close to me.

Things with Papa are improving, slowly but surely. I watch the care with which my mamma looks after him and I think, That is love.

The night we met, that same thought blinded me. You were there in front of me, and you were already everything.

I can't believe you don't want to hear from me.

What did I do?

Love,
Lucas

TO: amy.harlow@mercyhealth.com;
FROM: the.doc.mancini@gmail.com;
SUBJECT: Finding you again...

Dear Amy,

You don't know this, but I chased after you that first night. I was stunned into immobility when you ran away from me but when I saw the door shut behind you, I leapt into action. I almost caught you as well. You and Lilly had just gotten into that Uber when I reached you. And then you were gone.

Until you weren't. Imagine my surprise when you sat in front of me that Monday morning at that staff meeting. It rendered me mute with shock. There you were, the girl of my dreams, the girl I thought I'd never see again, working with me.

And then you hated me. Out of nowhere. You seemed to despise me right away and wow did that catch me off guard. I never understood what I did to deserve that. It doesn't matter now, I guess.

I want you to know that regardless of how this all turned out, finding you again that morning was one of the greatest miracles of my life.

Love,
Lucas

TO: amy.harlow@mercyhealth.com;
FROM: the.doc.mancini@gmail.com;
SUBJECT: That night

Dear Amy,

It's been eight months since that night and I still think about it. Still dream about it. When you agreed to get a midnight snack with me, I didn't want to blink in case you changed your mind. You were giving me a chance, and I wasn't going to waste it.

I know you won't read this but we never spoke about it and I haven't ever been able to say it. That night with you was the most amazing night I have ever spent with a woman.

You are it for me.

I wish I knew why you were blocking me.

I need to stop writing these emails.

TO: amy.harlow@mercyhealth.com;
FROM: the.doc.mancini@gmail.com;
SUBJECT: Coming home

Dear Amy,

My papa is doing better. He's up and about and can do more for himself. My parents have convinced me they will be fine if I return home. To you.

No, not to you.

I have spoken with Hector and he's happy to have me back in the emergency department at Mercy Hospital. I just need to decide if I want it. Do I want to see you again?

Stupid question. Of course, I do.

Do you want to see me again?

Only one way to find out.

Love,
Lucas

TO: amy.harlow@mercyhealth.com;
FROM: the.doc.mancini@gmail.com;
SUBJECT: Home.

Dear Amy,

I'm home. I just saw on Lilly's Instagram page she is having the grand opening of her café tomorrow. You must be so excited.

Given that you still appear to be blocking my every form of communication, I guess I'll pay the café a visit and try to clear the air.

Before we have to work together again.

Me coming back is probably a huge mistake but I have to try.

Don't I?

See you soon, Amy.

Love,
Lucas

After I have finished reading the emails, tears streaming down my face, I pull Snickers in for a tighter hug, trying to process everything that I've just read. Everything he'd so generously shared with me. I don't deserve it and I'm amazed that after everything I put him through, he still came back from Florence hoping for some clarity. Hoping to be with me.

As another sob is ripped out of me, I think of his face as I walked away from him earlier today. The look of devastation in his eyes as I chose my career and the opinion of others over him, and I'm gutted that I had treated him that way again. And yet he still came back to me this evening, heart in his hands. Wanting to make it right.

Without knowing what I did to deserve the love of such an amazing man, I sink back down into the couch and let myself wallow in my misery. All I know is that I need to fix it, to prove myself worthy of his love. But as I close my eyes and begin to fall asleep, I realise I don't have a clue where to start.

CHAPTER 25

With some good fortune—I was due some good luck—I have the rest of the week off work to help with the wedding preparations for the upcoming weekend. I give a silent thanks to the Amy from one month ago who had the good sense to book the time off. This gives me a couple of days to sit on the couch and lick my wounds while attempting to find a way to prove to Lucas just how much I love him. So far, a plan has eluded me, so I've stayed silent. Aware that he's waiting to hear from me, I have picked up the phone countless times to call him, only to be stumped by what to say if he were to pick up. I drafted hundreds of text messages, but they all sounded lame as well. After the emails Lucas let me read, I need my gesture to be grand. To be epic. And so, with no bright ideas, I decide to do nothing except wallow. That, I find, I am pretty good at.

Unfortunately, two days of self-pity is all I'm allowed as my parents blow back into town, ready for the big wedding weekend ahead. They decided to stay with me again, so I am afforded no space to cry in peace. My mum takes one look at me when she walks in the door and knows something is wrong. I guess my red-rimmed eyes and miserable demeanour isn't doing much to hide how I'm feeling.

"Tom, why don't you duck down to Lilly's café and get us some cupcakes?" she says after they've dropped their suitcases in my spare room, making themselves at home. Dad looks at me, gives me the biggest, warmest hug, and does what is asked of him. Which leaves me home alone with Mum. Yikes.

"Amy, dear. Tell me what's wrong. Is it Lucas?"

At the sound of his name, I cry again. I thought I would have run out of tears by now, but I was wrong. There are bucketloads of tears left to cry for that man.

"It's a mess, Mum. I've made a mess," I tell her between sobs.

She sits next to me on the couch, stroking my head and comforting me in the way only a mother can.

"Want to walk me through what's going on?" she says in a soft voice.

With an enormous sigh, I launch into everything that has transpired with Lucas over the last two years, including the fake dating, which causes my mum to huff and roll her eyes at me, culminating in the emails that he left for me to read. By the time I'm done, I'm emotionally spent.

"Really, Amy? Fake dating, lying to your parents?" she asks, looking a little miffed.

"Can you blame me? Ever since Oliver got engaged, you've been on a mission to marry me off to anybody that will take me. I had to do something."

"I haven't been that bad!"

"Benji?" I say, watching her face turn red at this reminder.

"Well, yes. You have a point. He was a little older than I expected," she concedes. "I just want you to be happy."

"Mum, what you don't realise is that I don't need a man to be happy. I've built a pretty good life for myself. By myself."

She nods and gives me a half smile. "I can see that now, and I'm sorry for pushing you to do something so crazy. But I have to say, you may have thought it was all pretend, but the man I met that weekend was in love with you."

My heart hurts hearing my mum say this, knowing that it's true. Or at least it was true at one point. Who knows whether Lucas can ever feel that way about me again? I say this to her, more tears streaming down my face.

"What if I've ruined everything? I told him we were done. I blamed him for things he didn't do. I've been awful," I sob, struggling to get the words out.

"Shhh, Amy," Mum soothes. "I saw how that man looked at you. He doesn't think you're awful. In fact, I think he thinks quite the opposite."

I feel myself fill with hope. "Even after the way I treated him at the hospital, he brought me the emails to read. And said that we should talk."

"So, why haven't you called him yet?" she demands, looking at me like I'm nuts.

"Because I don't know what to say! I need to fix everything, and it all feels overwhelming. And the wedding is tomorrow. I just can't seem to get my head right."

Mum gives me a stern look and says, "Amy Louise Harlow, you need to call that man and tell him how you feel. He has poured his heart out to you; you need to be brave and do the same for him."

I nod because she's right. I will call him, just not until after the wedding. If the conversation doesn't go well, I don't want to be a more heartbroken and sobbing mess than I already am. Lilly and

Oliver deserve more from me this weekend, and as maid of honour, I have to deliver.

That night, after spending the afternoon eating cupcakes with my parents and watching documentaries on the Discovery channel, I join Lilly and Snickers at her house for a sleepover. It's her last night as a single woman so we need to commemorate this occasion in style. Lilly has kicked Oliver out, sending him to spend the night at the house of his best man, Dale, and we have a movie marathon and a chocolate-eating fest all mapped out for us. I arrive, arms loaded with supplies; unicorn onesie pyjamas, face masks and only one bottle of wine. I cannot risk the two of us turning up to the wedding hungover. Because that totally sounds like something we would do.

"Come in, come in," Lilly says as she opens her front door, trying to hold Snickers back from his desperate attempts to escape. "I don't know what's wrong with him. Every time the door opens, he rushes out like he hates it here. One time he got out without us knowing and then we found him fifteen minutes later at the front door, knocking to come back in."

I lean down to give my quirky little furry friend a big hug, fending off his doggie kisses, and then straighten up to hug my best friend and soon-to-be sister-in-law.

"Happy last single-girl night!" I say, holding up all my goodies.

Lilly claps and jumps up and down. We haven't done a sleepover in the longest time.

"I have your favourite cookies cooling in the kitchen. The pizza is on the way. Let's get comfortable and get this slumber party started."

I show Lilly the novelty onesies that I have for us to wear and her face lights up in delight. Cute and comfortable; her dream outfit.

Once we're in our costumes for the evening, we sit on the couch with our modest glasses of wine, the pizza that's just arrived, and the cookies waiting for dessert. I couldn't envision a more perfect night.

"So, how are you doing Ames?" Lilly asks me as she takes a big bite of pizza, a long string of cheese dripping down her chin.

I hand her a napkin and sigh; this night should not be about me.

"I'm fine, Lil. Really," I add when she gives me a doubtful look. "This weekend is all about you. We can deal with the car wreck that is my love life when you're back from your honeymoon."

Lilly and Oliver have two weeks planned at a romantic resort in Fiji and I know she's looking forward to that more than she is to the wedding.

"I love that you want to focus on me, Ames. But I know you, I know you're hurting. And Lucas, he's hurting, too." She says this last part with such conviction that my spidey senses go off.

"How do you know what Lucas is feeling?" I ask.

As I watch her, she looks very interested in the pizza slice in front of her all of a sudden, frowning as she picks off a piece of mushroom and avoiding both my eyes and my question.

"Lilly Hamilton, soon to be Harlow. What have you done?"

She lets out a big sigh, her face turning pink, and finally looks at me.

"I may have had a teeny, tiny chat with Lucas the other day."

"You did WHAT?" I scream.

"Just a little chat, the day you guys had that blow-up? I thought maybe you needed a little help, you know? Like how you stepped in and helped me and Ollie?" she says, looking very sheepish.

I think about what she's saying as realisation dawns on me. "Was this just before he dropped off the emails?"

Lilly nods, a small smile on her face. "I didn't know he was going to do that," she says. "I just gave your outburst some context and he did the rest."

"Context? You told him about James?" I ask, my face heating with mortification.

"Well, someone had to! You should have told him months ago. Years ago. The poor guy has been paying for James's mistakes and he didn't even know it." She took a big sip of wine and held eye contact with me. Wow, I didn't know that Lilly felt so strongly about this.

"I agree," I say, shocking the both of us. "And I'm grateful that you had that conversation with him. Thank you, Lilly."

Lilly's eyes fill with tears as she hugs me. "I'm so glad you aren't mad at me. I just felt like I needed to do something. He's your perfect match and I want you to be happy. But that's it, now I'm out. The two of you need to sort this out by yourselves."

"Well, firstly, thanks for being such a good friend and trying to fix my love life the week before your wedding," I say, leaning over to give her a big hug. "And secondly, I think that it's on me to sort this whole mess out. He has shown me his cards. It's my turn now."

"So, what's the plan?" Lilly asks the million-dollar question.

"Bestie, I don't have a clue."

The next morning, I wake up in Lilly's bed. We spent the rest of the evening giving ourselves facials, painting our nails and watching 90s romantic comedies. It was the perfect last night. And now today, Lilly is getting married. I look over to where she's still sleeping, so happy for her it hurts. No one deserves happiness more than her, and today works for me as well. I am not losing a best friend but gaining a sister.

"I can feel you staring at me," she mumbles, her eyes still closed.

"Happy wedding day!" I yell, more of a morning person than my friend.

"Shhh, still sleeping," she says, pulling the pillow up over her ears, keeping her eyes firmly shut.

"I'm giving you five more minutes to sleep while I make us coffee. And then it's time to get you up. And get you married!" I'm so excited, I all but bounce out of bed.

As I'm making the coffee, I assemble a platter of pastries and fruit—my feeble attempt at "cooking" Lilly breakfast—and by the time she stumbles down the stairs, still in her unicorn onesie, I have it all laid out for her.

"You are the best maid of honour ever," she says, taking the coffee from me, her eyes slowly focusing.

I pick my list up off the table and tell her what needs to be done this morning, as she groans and nibbles on some fruit.

"That sounds like a lot of work," she says when I am only halfway through my list.

"Then we'd better get started. You need to shower while I steam your dress. The hair and make-up team will be here in thirty minutes. Let's go, go, go."

Lilly looks like she may hate me at this moment, but she does as she is told, while I answer the door and let the florist in with all the bouquets for the day. It's starting!

After a few hours and many complaints from Lilly later, we're ready to go. I stare at my best friend in front of me, and my eyes well with tears.

"You're the most beautiful bride I have ever seen," I tell her, dabbing at my eyes and trying not to ruin my expertly made-up face.

Lilly looks at herself in the mirror and smiles. The dress fits her body perfectly, and with her hair half up in a simple style complete with a few fresh flowers, she looks like herself, just a more polished version.

"Do not even think about eating or drinking anything," I tell her as we wait for the car to pick us up and take us to the chapel. Lilly is renowned for spilling just about everything and we cannot take the risk with her beautiful, crisp white wedding dress.

"You're no fun today," she says, smiling at me. "But I can't imagine doing this without you. And you look amazing. That dress was a wonderful choice."

Lilly and I had spent countless hours searching for the lilac strapless gown I'm wearing today. It's body-hugging, with some ruching on the sides, falling to the ground with a thigh-high slit. It's sexier than your average maid of honour gown, but when we saw it, Lilly was determined that I should have it. I've styled it with strappy silver heels, and have left my hair down long and straight, parted in the middle. Looking at the two of us today, I think back to the day we met in kindergarten and cannot believe how far we've come.

"If I don't have time to tell you later, you're the best friend a girl could ever ask for. And I'm so happy you're marrying my brother today," I tell her.

Lilly blubbers a bit at this, slightly ruining her mascara, while she pulls me in for a hug. "I love you, Amy."

"I love you, too. Now let's get you married!"

CHAPTER 26

NINETY MINUTES LATER, I WATCH as the celebrant declares Lilly and Oliver man and wife. I clap loudly and wipe the tears that have been forming for the entire ceremony as the two of them have their first kiss. When Lilly emerges, her cheeks are flushed and she looks radiant. Turning to me, she gives me a big hug before taking her bouquet and making her way down the aisle, her husband by her side.

I take Dale's offered arm and we follow them out of the chapel where we're soon surrounded by well-wishers, all wanting to take a photo with the married couple and their bridal party. As we're posing for photo number 1,008, I look up to see a gorgeous man leaning against a tree, watching it all play out, a small smile on his face. *Lucas.*

Shocked, I look at him again, and then turn to look at Lilly, who's grinning at me.

"I know I said I wouldn't interfere again, but I couldn't resist," she says, looking not one bit apologetic.

"You asked him to come?"

"I did," she confirms, giving me a little push toward him. "Now go talk to him."

I look to where Lucas is waiting for me and nerves fill my stomach. "What about the wedding photos?" I ask, stalling for time.

"Go!" Lilly says, pointing at Lucas and then turning around to ignore me. So, I guess I'm going to talk to Lucas.

As I walk toward him, he straightens up from his leaning position, his eyes running up and down my body. My knees wobble a bit as I get closer but I steel my spine, determined to do this. He deserves for me to be the brave one.

"Lucas," I breathe out when I get to him. "Hi."

Lucas gives me a nervous smile, making me melt a little. He leans forward and brushes his lips against my cheek. "You look beautiful, Amy," he whispers next to my ear.

Lost for what to say in response to this, I take a moment to stare at him. He's wearing a black suit with a crisp white shirt and a blue tie to match his eyes. And he looks magnificent.

"Thanks for coming," I say, like we're meeting for afternoon tea.

"Lilly said it would be alright," he replies, looking uncertain. So different from the confident person he normally is.

"Sorry I haven't called," I blurt out, unable to have him looking so uncomfortable.

His cheeks heat to a shade of pink and he clears his throat. "You didn't have to call."

"But I wanted to," I tell him in a firm voice, hoping to get through to him. "I just didn't know what to say."

His cheeks flush a deeper shade of red. "I know those emails were a lot..."

"No! That's not it. I loved the emails, I loved reading them," I tell him, watching his eyes light up with this information. "I just felt like I needed to do something equally monumental in return."

"So that's why you didn't call. You wanted to wait for...?" he says, sounding confused.

"I wanted to do a grand gesture," I confess, feeling all kinds of stupid. "You deserve a grand gesture."

Lucas moves closer to me, causing me to shiver in response. Upon seeing this, he frowns and shrugs out of his jacket, putting it over my shoulders and closing the lapels together in front of me, coming ever so close in the process.

"Thanks," I say, breathing in the scent of him from his jacket.

"So, about this grand gesture, what does it look like?"

"I don't know," I say, shrugging in response. "I was thinking about turning up at your house with a big 'please forgive me' sign. Or attempting to make another viral video where I declare my feelings for you. Or something else just as stupid."

Lucas laughs, his face filled with happiness as I stand there looking at him in awe.

"About these feelings you were so eager to share?" he says, his words teasing, but his voice serious.

With a deep breath, I look him straight in the eye. "I'm so in love with you, Lucas. I think I have been since the day we met."

Before the last word is out of my mouth, Lucas has his lips on mine, pressing on me a kiss filled with every emotion he's feeling. The kiss is not gentle and I match his intensity with my own. One of his hands cradles my jaw while the other is on my lower back, pulling me closer to him and eliciting a small moan from the back of my throat. The kiss goes on and on, shattering every other kiss that came before it.

"I love you too," he says when we finally come up for air, his voice rough. "So much."

At this confession, I reach up and smatter kisses all over his face, unable to contain my joy. This amazing man standing here in front of me is still in love with me! When I finish assaulting his eyes, his mouth, his cheeks, which he seems to delight in, I lean back in his arms, serious once again.

"I'm so sorry for everything I've done to hurt you, Lucas," I tell him, putting every ounce of sincerity I have into my voice.

"I know you are, Ames. And I understand. And I forgive you."

"You do?" I asked, shocked, having expected to work harder to gain his forgiveness. "Because I think I definitely owe you a grand gesture or two in the future."

Lucas shakes his head and gives me a bemused smile before pulling me closer and tucking me in under his chin. With a deep sigh, he whispers, "I don't need a grand gesture. I have everything I need right here."

I lean back to look into his deep blue eyes, ready for another earth-shattering kiss.

"My, dear, sorry to interrupt," Mum says from somewhere nearby, not looking at all sorry to be interrupting. In fact, she looks giddy with happiness. Similar to what I must look like if I'm honest. "But Lilly can't hold off the photographer for much longer."

I bite my lip, knowing that I need to get back to my duties as maid of honour, but loathing the idea of letting Lucas go. Even if it's just for the night.

"You go," Lucas says, reading the reluctance on my face. "I'll see you in a bit at the reception."

My head whips back to his, where he's grinning at me. "What?" I ask, confused and oh-so-happy.

"Lilly invited me," he says, his smile growing in size as he takes in my gleeful grin. "So, I'll see you soon."

I look over to where Lilly, my matchmaking fairy godmother, is watching and blowing me kisses and I'm overwhelmed. With tears filling my eyes—again—I blow kisses back to her, before turning to Lucas and giving him another kiss for the road. When we both come back for air, his cheeks are red, his eyes glazed, and neither of us looks like we want to be going to a wedding.

"Amy! Come on," Mum badgers me, losing patience with us.

"Coming, Mum," I say, placing another soft kiss on the mouth of the man I love. "I'll see you soon."

Lucas smiles, giving me one last squeeze.

"I'll be waiting."

Several hours later, we've eaten, danced, given speeches, cut the cake, and the wedding is now winding down. Much to my delight, Lilly seated Lucas next to me at the bridal table, so I've been able to spend most of the evening wrapped up in his arms. With the air now cleared between us, he seems unable to keep his hands to himself. Not that I'm complaining I'm also struggling not to throw myself at him at any opportunity.

With the band announcing the last song of the night, Lucas stands up and offers me his hand. I follow him out onto the dance floor and step into his arms, snuggling in close against his chest, his arms strong bands behind my back.

"You don't know how long I've waited to be with you like this," Lucas says in a soft voice.

I lean back ever so slightly and give him a small smile. "Oh, I think I can imagine. I've been fighting my feelings for you for what feels like forever."

Lucas rewards this little fact with a brief but passionate kiss, his arms pressing me even closer, until there isn't a sliver of daylight between us.

"I wish you hadn't fought it so hard," he says.

"I know, me too," I tell him, filled with regret over the time we've wasted when we could have been together. Like this.

"I guess we'll just have to make up for lost time," he says, reading my thoughts and giving me a mischievous grin.

"And how do you propose we do that?" I say, feeling flirty and lighter than I have in years.

"I can think of a few things," he says in that gravelly voice, leaning in closer for one more kiss—

"Ouch!" I say as I feel something heavy and prickly hit me in the head. "What the—?"

I look down to see Lilly's bouquet at my feet, where she'd thrown it deliberately at me, clearly thinking she hadn't 100 per cent completed her role as matchmaker. Lucas leans down to pick it up and hands it to me with a bow while everyone cheers around us. With my face in the flowers to hide my flaming cheeks, I look at Lilly who is mouthing "I love you" from her spot on the stage and then back to Lucas, who is watching me with adoration written all over his face, and I'm ready to burst with happiness. How did I get so lucky?

"Looks like you two will be next," Mum says, as she and Dad dance past us.

"Mum!" I yell, my cheeks getting even hotter. "Sorry about that," I mumble to Lucas, mortified by what has taken place around me.

"Don't be," Lucas says, his eyes soft and his voice serious. "I intend to make this a reality one day soon. You are my forever, Amy Harlow. And I know I will love you, for always."

For always, I think as I settle back into his arms. That has a nice ring to it.

The End

EPILOGUE

Lucas

Florence—Three Months Later

I WATCH MAMMA AND ISABELLA in the kitchen attempting to teach Amy how to make fresh gnocchi, and my heart feels full. With Amy here meeting my family for the first time, and fitting in with everyone so effortlessly, it's as though the last piece of the puzzle has been put into place.

During the last three months, our relationship has grown into something even better than my wildest dreams. And believe me, I've had many a dream about Amy. Shortly after Lilly and Oliver's wedding, we went to HR at the hospital and disclosed our relationship. I told Hector to take me off the committee involved in the hiring of the Chief Nursing Officer position, and with the help of Janine from HR, we've had a smooth transition in the emergency department, with most of our colleagues happy that we are "finally" together. It took Amy a little while to adjust to our new reality, and she has insisted that we act professionally at work, which is fine with me because having to keep my hands off her all day at the hospital makes reuniting with her in the evening even sweeter.

Four weeks ago, Amy interviewed for the new role and crushed it. From what I heard, there was no competition. Two days later, they offered her the role and there wasn't a single person prouder of her than me. I took her out to dinner that night, and she kept looking at me expectantly the whole evening. I suspect the little sneak has seen the ring that I'd bought for her (the day after we got together) and she's now on pins and needles every time she thinks we're having a romantic moment.

It's been fun playing with her a bit. Planning romantic picnics and not proposing. A day trip to the snow, no proposal. I'm pretty sure that after a month of non-proposals, Amy has given up hope of it happening anytime soon, which is fine with me. This means that when I take her into the city of Florence tomorrow, to "show her the sights," it will actually be a surprise when I get down on one knee with the whole Florence skyline as our backdrop. It feels like the perfect place to do it—there isn't a prettier city than Florence.

"You look happy, son," my papa says, coming up behind me, standing with me to watch the three women in our lives bonding in the kitchen.

"I am," I tell him with full sincerity. The time I have spent with Amy has made me happier than I ever thought I could be.

"Good, good," he says, patting my shoulder. "Does this mean you aren't ever moving home?" he asks, his eyes a little sad.

"I'll come back to visit often, Papa. But you have to know now that Amy is my home," I tell him, giving him a side hug.

Amy is my always.

If you loved Always, Amy, it would mean the world to me if you could leave a review or a rating on a site like, Amazon, Goodreads or wherever you review books.

Reviews mean so much to authors and could very well be the motivation needed to keep writing, and to publish that next novel.

Want to know what Lucas was thinking at the bachelor/bachelorette party where they 'finally' kiss again? Go to my website and sign up to my newsletter for a FREE BONUS CHAPTER.

Isabella's story (book three in the Love Always series) will be available late 2023. Read on to see where her story begins...

ISABELLA

I'M CRAMMED IN THE BACK seat of Lucas's hired Mini Cooper as we zoom the forty minutes from our small village toward the city of Florence. Lucas has insisted I join them today, to act as a decoy in case Amy becomes suspicious of the true nature of our excursion, and also to play the role of photographer to capture their perfect proposal moment.

From my vantage point in the back of the car, I watch as my brother picks up Amy's hand and places a soft kiss on it, and sigh. I'm so happy for the two of them, and I love Amy, having become fast friends with her since their arrival four days ago, but I'm also bursting with envy.

Amy is my age, and here she is travelling the world with the man she loves, about to get engaged in one of the most romantic cities in the world, while I spend my time sitting at home watching Netflix with my parents every night. Don't get me wrong, I love my parents and am happy to live near them and help them run their deli, especially since Papa got sick last year, but there's a part of me, a part that's getting bigger every day, that yearns for something more.

Since Lucas moved to Melbourne over two years ago, I've been fascinated with the place. I follow his sporadic posts on Instagram with an unhealthy obsession, which has only increased since he got together with Amy and her social media presence has doubled his. I obsess over their nights out in funky bars, at the theatre and live music, even at a game of something they call "footy," which looks nothing like our football, because the players, bizarrely, can use their hands. Every time I get notified of one of their posts, I'm filled with a longing to get on a plane and see it all for myself, but I'm not even brave enough to broach the subject of me leaving with my parents, let alone actually flying all the way to the other side of the world to have my own adventures.

"Bella? We're here." Lucas's voice brings me back from my inner musings. "I'm just going to take Amy up to the lookout to show her the view. You can wander around and meet us back here, *bene?*" he says, slipping into Italian and giving me a meaningful look, making sure I understand the plan. The plan is for me to follow close behind them and hide in the bushes, ready to take a photo of Lucas down on one knee. *Let's hope she says yes,* I think to myself with a smile.

"Bella?" Lucas repeats my name, sounding nervous.

"*Si,*" I reply quickly. "Yes. You go, I'll meet you later. Have fun, Amy." I give her a hug before they walk away.

I follow behind them at a careful distance and position myself in the perfect spot. And with my camera furiously clicking, I watch as my brother proposes to the love of his life. With tears of happiness running down my face, I watch as Amy says an emphatic "yes!" and reflect on my role here today with a sense of melancholy. That of the observer. And finally, something snaps in me. I have to take control of my life. It's time I stop watching it go by from the sidelines. It's time for me to have adventures of my own. It's in this moment, standing in the city I have lived my entire life, that I decide I am going to Melbourne.

ACKNOWLEDGEMENTS

To the person who believes in me the most, my partner in all of this and my love, Philip. You have been by my side since we started this crazy journey and you have worked so hard to make this dream a reality for me. I don't think I have enough words to thank you for all that you do for me. I love you so much. And to Hunter and Sienna, thank you for putting up with a mummy who sometimes gets lost in the fictional world in her laptop. The two of you are what makes anything I do in life worthwhile, and I love you more than I have the words to say.

To my editor, Britt. Your work on this book has been invaluable, and I don't think I would have got it right without you. I'm looking forward to working with you again soon! To Lorissa, for the most beautiful covers for both my novels, I cannot thank you enough for bringing my visions to life so masterfully. It has been a joy working with you. And to my beta readers, Brittnei and Emma, you both gave me the early hope that maybe my book isn't complete garbage. Thank you!

To my family and friends who have been so supportive of Love, Lilly and this adventure I'm taking. Thank you all for going out and quietly buying the book, even if it's not something you would normally read. I hope you enjoyed this one! Your support is so important to me, so thank you.

To my readers, thank you for the enthusiasm you've had for my writing. For encouraging me to keep going with every kind word, every Pinterest board and every Instagram post. I hope you enjoyed this book and that you're looking forward to the next one (it's so good!)

And finally, to my parents. I want to thank you both for everything you've ever given me. My entire life you've both worked hard to make sure I've had everything I've ever needed. You raised me to believe I can do and be anything I put my mind to and I wouldn't be the person I am today without you. I love you both very much.

Love Always,
Belinda

ABOUT THE AUTHOR

Belinda Mary has dreamed of being a writer her whole life. And after many, many years of excuses and procrastination, she has taken the leap and is finally ready to share some stories. Belinda is a long-time lover of all the books, and when she is not reading or writing, she can be found spending time with her family she adores, watching all things Bravo, or listening to true crime podcasts. Belinda hopes to write the kind of stories that she loves to read; filled with laughter, longing and love.

You can find out more about Belinda and connect with her online and on social media.

@belindamary *@belindamary*

@belindamary.author *@belindamary.author*

www.belindamary.com

Printed in Great Britain
by Amazon